CRITTERS OF AOTEAROA

CRITTERS OF AOTEAROA

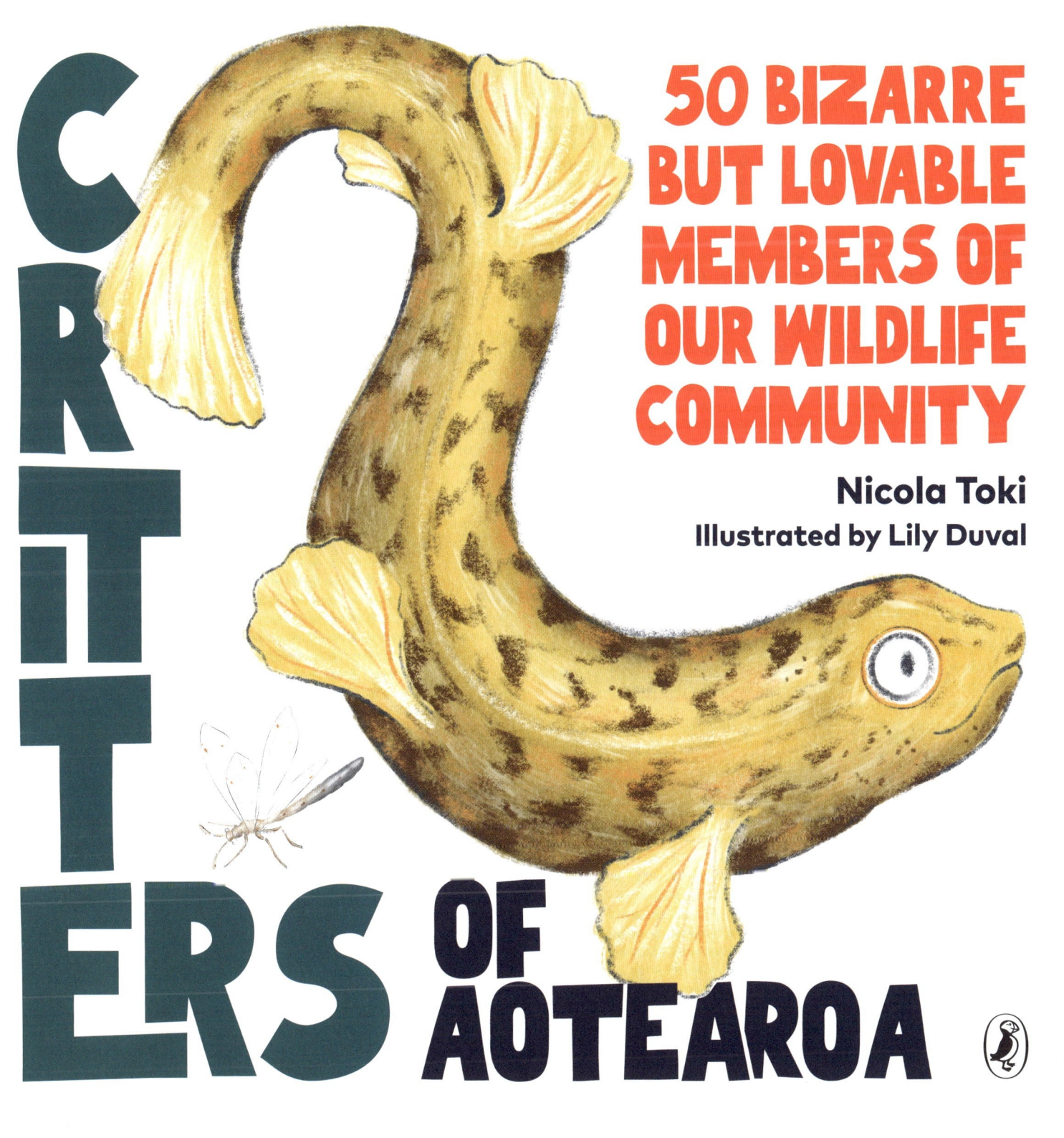

50 BIZARRE BUT LOVABLE MEMBERS OF OUR WILDLIFE COMMUNITY

Nicola Toki

Illustrated by Lily Duval

CONTENTS

Introduction
Jesse Mulligan
PAGE 7

Antipodes Island parakeet
PAGE 8

Archey's frog
PAGE 10

Blobfish
PAGE 12

Bryde's whale
PAGE 14

Cicadas/Kihikihi/Tātarakihi
PAGE 16

Cook Strait giant wētā
PAGE 18

Crimson jellyfish
PAGE 20

Dog vomit slime mould
PAGE 22

Forest ringlet butterfly
PAGE 24

Freshwater bristle worm
PAGE 26

Giant knobbled weevil
PAGE 28

Glow-in-the-dark freshwater snail limpet
PAGE 30

Greta Thunberg freshwater snail
PAGE 32

Hagfish
PAGE 34

Harlequin gecko
PAGE 36

Helms' stag beetle
PAGE 38

Horrid stick insect
PAGE 40

Huhu
PAGE 42

Katipō spider
PAGE 44

Kupe's grass moth
PAGE 46

Leaf-veined slug
PAGE 48

Long-tailed bat
PAGE 50

Longfin eel/Tuna
PAGE 52

Mantis shrimp
PAGE 54

Marsh crake/Koitareke
PAGE 56

Mercury Islands tusked wētā
PAGE 58

Native mole cricket
PAGE 60

New Zealand antlion/Kutu kutu
PAGE 62

New Zealand glow worm
PAGE 64

New Zealand lamprey
PAGE 66

New Zealand pea crab
PAGE 68

Nudibranchs
PAGE 70

Peripatus/Ngāokeoke/ Velvet worm/ Walking worm
PAGE 72

Rangatira spider
PAGE 74

Robust grasshopper
PAGE 76

Seabird tick
PAGE 78

Sea squirt or Sea tulip/Kaeo
PAGE 80

Sinbad skink
PAGE 82

Six-eyed spider
PAGE 84

Smeagol the gravel maggot
PAGE 86

Striped skink
PAGE 88

Tadpole shrimp/ Shield shrimp
PAGE 90

Tardigrades
PAGE 92

Tea-tree fingers
PAGE 94

Teviot flathead galaxias
PAGE 96

Vegetable sheep
PAGE 98

Wandering sea anemone
PAGE 100

Wrybill/Ngutu pare/ Ngutu parore
PAGE 102

Yellow octopus
PAGE 104

Zebra moth/ South Island lichen moth
PAGE 106

Critter quiz
PAGE 108

Index
PAGE 114

About Nic
PAGE 116

About Lily
PAGE 117

Acknowledgements
PAGE 118

Answers
PAGE 119

INTRODUCTION

New Zealand wildlife has a problem: the better an animal looks, the more people want to save it. Or, to put it another way, nobody cares about you if you're ugly.

Banks and airlines and chocolate companies line up to give money to the cute animals: the kākāpō and dolphins of this world. That's fine, but there are thousands of other less cuddly creatures who are just as important to our natural world but who have trouble interesting corporate sponsors and, dare I say it, ordinary nature-loving Kiwis.

That's why Nicola Toki and I started 'Critter of the Week', a weekly radio series where we highlight the lesser-known, lesser-loved native animals — one slimy, scaly, occasionally smelly species at a time. We've been doing it for almost 10 years and we're in no danger of running out (New Zealand has about 4000 species listed as 'threatened'), though there have been times when Nic's been part-way through describing the latest act of insect eroto-cannibalism and I've thought: 'How long will they let us get away with this?'

Our listeners love 'Critter of the Week', and over the years we've given them opportunities to share their enthusiasm with us. We had a critter cake competition, a 'knit-a-critter' contest and sold thousands of t-shirts that people can proudly wear to advertise the fact they care about the little (ugly) guys.

And now here is the book. Congratulations! Just by owning one you're helping shine a spotlight into the dark, slithery corners of New Zealand's awesome nature scene. Each profile features a beautiful illustration by Lily Duval, a warts-and-all description from Nicola and a brutally honest rating on the attractiveness-ometer (remember, the lower the better — this ain't no beauty contest).

We hope you learn to love these underdogs as much as we do. They may not be cute, but each has a secret life so wonderfully interesting, you'll realise that nature's best stories are the ones you have to work a little harder to uncover.

Jesse Mulligan

RNZ TE REO IRIRANGI O AOTEAROA

YOU DON'T HAVE TO GO TO THE ANTIPODES ISLANDS TO SEE THEM — THERE ARE BIRDS LIVING IN CAPTIVITY IN ZOOS AND WILDLIFE PARKS ACROSS NEW ZEALAND.

IT IS THE ONLY NATIVE PARAKEET WITH AN ENTIRELY GREEN HEAD.

CRITTER ATTRACTIVENESS-OMETER

7.5

PROBABLY 8.5, IF IT WASN'T FOR ITS SLIGHTLY EVIL-LOOKING ORANGE EYES.

ANTIPODES ISLAND PARAKEET

The Antipodes Island parakeet, *Cyanoramphus unicolor*, is one of our native species of kākāriki. It's larger than most of our other parakeets. And it's a remarkable bright green, with a lovely two-coloured beak. In some ways it looks like a shrunk-down version of a kākāpō.

You'd have to get on a boat to go and see this critter in the wild, because it's found only on the Antipodes Islands, deep in the Southern Ocean. It's pretty cute, but some of its eating habits are a bit gross.

What's neat about these parakeets is that, on the Antipodes Islands — way down in the subantarctic, in the Roaring Forties (between the latitudes of 40 to 50 degrees south), with its wild weather — they live in burrows underground, up to 1 metre long (presumably for protection from the climate), and although they can fly, they hop around in the tussock to find food. Very cute! But what's not so cute is that they are carrion feeders, which means they eat dead animals.

Scientists discovered that as well as eating leaves and seeds, the parakeets were picking away at rotting carcasses to add extra protein to their diet. They scavenge the corpses of dead albatrosses and penguins, and have also occasionally even been seen attacking and killing little seabirds and eating them underground, like wild vampire parakeets!

Today there are probably somewhere between 2000 and 3000 birds in the wild. Their populations were being affected quite seriously by mice until 2018, when these rodents were successfully eradicated from the Antipodes Islands. The islands are more than 800 kilometres southeast of Rakiura/Stewart Island and are about 2000 hectares in size, so getting rid of thousands of mice from an environment that large, stark and extreme was a significant achievement.

Were the mice killing the adult birds? No — the problem was that the mice were competing with the parakeets for food. They were eating all of the things that an Antipodes Island parakeet needed to survive. The Antipodes Island parakeet is now doing very nicely, which is pretty great.

ARCHEY'S FROG

ARCHEY'S FROGS DON'T HAVE EXTERNAL EARDRUMS LIKE OTHER FROGS, SO THEY DON'T COMMUNICATE BY CROAKING — THEY RECEIVE SIGNALS FROM OTHER FROGS USING THEIR SENSE OF SMELL.

There is something very cute about frogs — many people have a real affinity with them. A lot of it has to do with memories of collecting tadpoles from a local drain or pond and watching them transform into tiny frogs. But that's not the case with our Archey's frogs, because they don't even have tadpoles!

Archey's frog (*Leiopelma archeyi*) is one of three native species of frogs. It doesn't live in ponds or rivers — it's terrestrial, living in the bush. It doesn't even have webbing between its long toes, because it doesn't need to swim. It doesn't live in pools of water, so neither do its babies. Instead, the females lay their eggs in a nice, damp spot somewhere in the bush, and then it's a solo dad situation. Out of the eggs

NEW ZEALAND NATIVE FROGS HAVE ONE ADDITIONAL VERTEBRA THAT OTHER FROGS DON'T HAVE.

CRITTER ATTRACTIVENESS-OMETER: 8

FOR ITS BEAUTIFUL ROUND EYES AND PAINTED MARKINGS.

hatch tiny little froglets (one of the cutest things in the universe), which climb up on their dad's back and he carries them around for a couple of weeks, until they are big enough to live on their own.

Archey's frogs are really beautiful, and also fascinating. They are almost identical to frog fossils from 150 million years ago, and what that means is that frogs like these were literally hopping around the feet of dinosaurs.

They may have once hopped over much larger areas of Aotearoa, too, but sadly they're now only found in a tiny little patch of bush west of Te Kuiti and also on the Coromandel Peninsula. Loss of habitat and introduced predators, like rats, have seriously reduced their numbers. In fact, on the list of the world's EDGE species — EDGE stands for Evolutionarily Distinct and Globally Endangered — Archey's frog has the dubious honour of being the number-one amphibian.

Frogs can be described as 'the canary in the coal mine' — indicators of whether an ecosystem is healthy. Frogs have incredibly sensitive skin, so if their environment is polluted or other environmental factors are out of balance, frogs will not survive, which is a really big red flag that something is wrong.

Internationally, many species of frog have been affected by the chytrid fungus, which infects their skin and can kill them. But our native frogs, and particularly Archey's frog, are able to cure themselves — somehow, very quickly, the secretions in their skin are able to get rid of the chytrid fungus. That's incredible! Perhaps it's to do with how long they have been isolated from other frogs, or perhaps they've turned into super-frogs over 150 million years of evolution.

Archey's frogs are really difficult to find, but they don't move around a lot — if you saw one in the bush under a rock and went back a year later, there's a good chance it would still be under the same rock! You can help protect these frogs — if you find one, make sure you report it through the DOC (Department of Conservation) website.

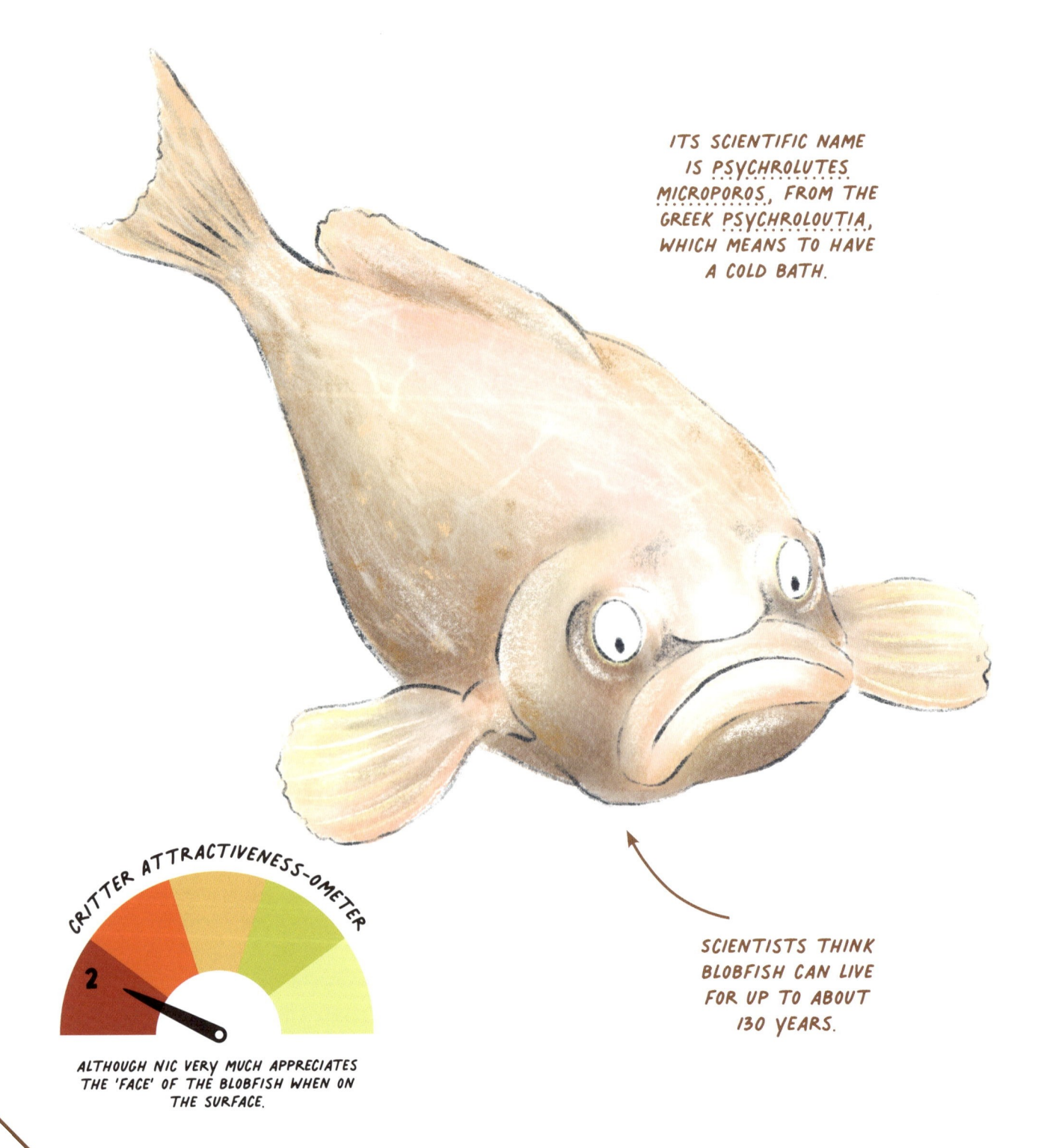

ITS SCIENTIFIC NAME IS PSYCHROLUTES MICROPOROS, FROM THE GREEK PSYCHROLOUTIA, WHICH MEANS TO HAVE A COLD BATH.

SCIENTISTS THINK BLOBFISH CAN LIVE FOR UP TO ABOUT 130 YEARS.

CRITTER ATTRACTIVENESS-OMETER

2

ALTHOUGH NIC VERY MUCH APPRECIATES THE 'FACE' OF THE BLOBFISH WHEN ON THE SURFACE.

BLOBFISH

Cute animals always get the best press, don't they? As humans, we tend to assign animals human characteristics in their appearance and behaviour (anthropomorphism), and sometimes treat them as if they *are* human. That means we also label them as pretty or ugly. And there is none more ugly than the blobfish. When it's out of the water, it almost looks like something you might sneeze up. It is a sort of gelatinous mass with two little eyes and big lips. In 2013 it was voted the world's ugliest animal!

Unfortunately, what also often happens is that we go all-out to protect the cute things — and then pay much less attention to things that are not so lovely to look at. But we should think again. Despite their unlovely appearance, blobfish have incredible superpowers.

They live in the abyssal zones (deep, deep areas under the sea) of oceans around Australia and New Zealand, and have been found more than 1 kilometre below the surface. They live at a level nearly 10 times as deep as most of the other sea life that we're aware of, in complete darkness. Yet somehow they've been able to survive and thrive in places that for us would be like trying to live on the moon.

Impressively, the squidgy-looking blobfish can be an ambush predator, like the tuatara — they sit and wait then pounce on things that come too close to their mouth. The blobfish can catch crabs, lobsters, sea urchins and other molluscs, as well as eating dead stuff. They're super zen, sitting very still, and don't expend energy unless they absolutely have to!

When they're in their natural environment, their bodies have to cope with enormous amounts of pressure from all the water pushing down from above, so they've evolved to deal with that. They're 'blobby' — their bones are really, really soft, so that they don't break or crack under the pressure. In fact, the pressure is what's holding them together.

Their gelatinous flesh is slightly less dense than seawater, which is basically how they're able to stay afloat down there. When they're pulled up to the surface — often through fishing methods like bottom-trawling, as well as by scientific expeditions — their physical appearance completely changes. They essentially deflate, going from looking like a fish to being a jelly-like blob.

When they're swimming in the dark ocean, deep beneath the surface, they don't have that big proboscis (that nose-looking thing) that they have when we pull them up. So the message there is: in their home environment, they might in fact be quite beautiful!

BRYDE'S WHALE

Bryde's whale (*Balaenoptera brydei*) is worthy of a mention because most people probably haven't heard of it. Its name is pronounced 'brooders'. They're called a tropical whale because they like warmer waters — living between 40 degrees north and 40 degrees south of the equator.

Despite being high up on the endangered list (their status is 'nationally critical'), they're often seen at sea, especially in the waters of the Hauraki Gulf. And there's a really good reason for that — although these things are *enormous*, they spend 90 per cent of their life between the surface and 15 metres underwater. They like to hang out near the top of the ocean, which of course is where the people are. Great for spotting . . . but the downside sometimes is coming off second best in encounters with boats, especially big ones.

Despite their stupendous size — this baleen whale grows up to 15 metres long, roughly the length of three giraffes lined up end to end, and can weigh as much as seven elephants, about 40,000 kilograms — they're filter feeders, eating plankton, tiny fish and maybe krill. To gather their food, they use a technique we call 'lunge feeding': they roll on their side with their mouth wide open and gulp in seawater, then they push the water back out through the bony baleen plates in their mouth, like a sieve. The fish and the krill get caught in the baleen, and can then be swallowed.

Because they spend so much time near the ocean's surface, the main threat to Bryde's whales is being hit by ships, like the container vessels that pass in and out of Auckland's port. A lot of research has been done on how to avoid this happening, but basically it really helps if ships slow down in areas where there are whales about!

And this is probably a good opportunity to remind everyone that we do have some clear rules for anyone engaging with whales at sea in New Zealand. The law says you must stay at least 50 metres away from any whale; you must stay 200 metres away from any whale mother and calf; you're certainly not allowed to swim with whales (there are all kinds of health and safety reasons for that); and if you're on a boat, make sure that you're not approaching the whale head on, cutting across their path or getting in their way. We're not saying don't enjoy your time with whales — just do it politely!

BRYDE'S WHALES ARE NAMED AFTER A NORWEGIAN WHALER, JOHAN BRYDE, WHO ESTABLISHED EARLY WHALING STATIONS IN SOUTH AFRICA.

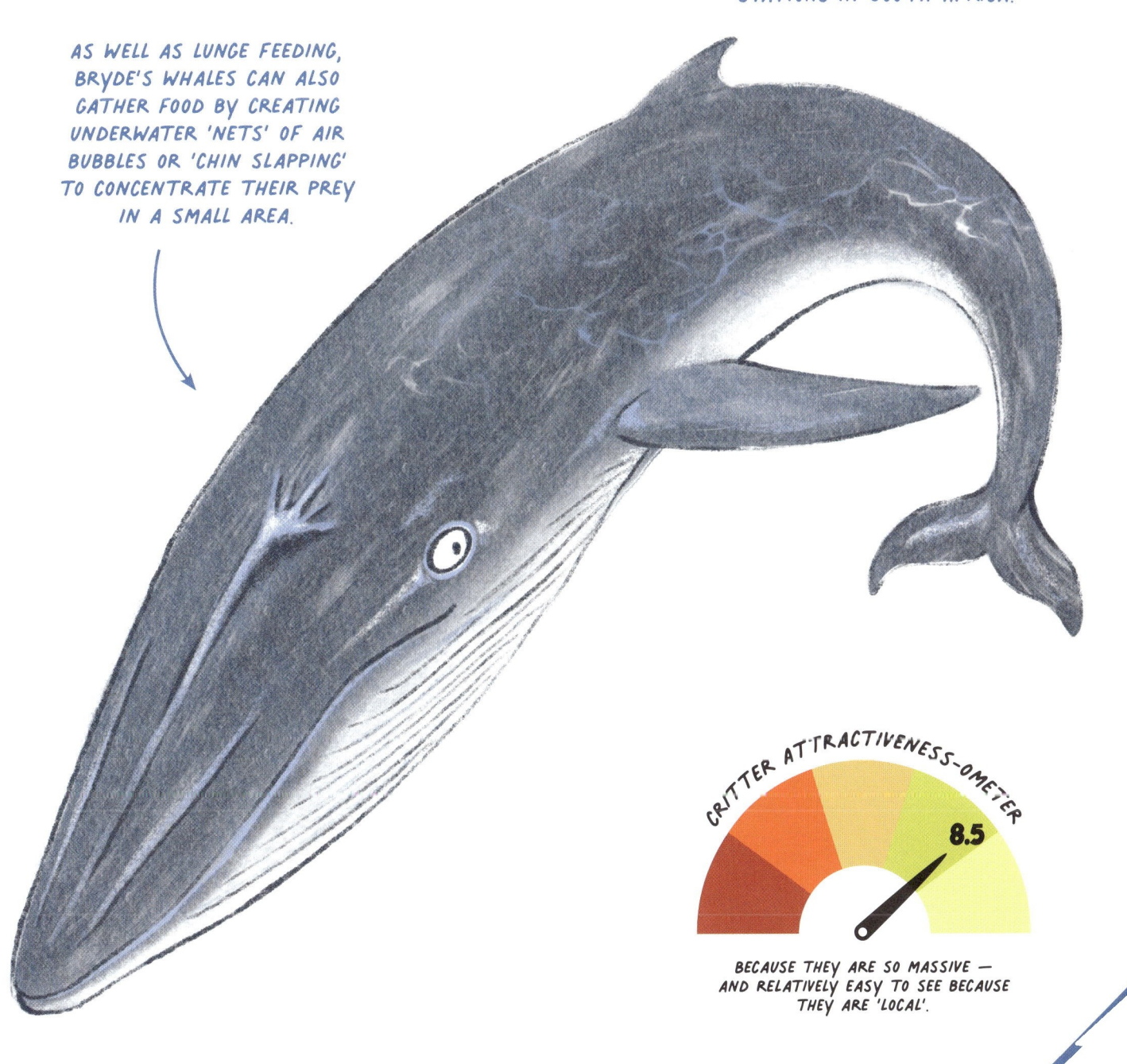

AS WELL AS LUNGE FEEDING, BRYDE'S WHALES CAN ALSO GATHER FOOD BY CREATING UNDERWATER 'NETS' OF AIR BUBBLES OR 'CHIN SLAPPING' TO CONCENTRATE THEIR PREY IN A SMALL AREA.

CRITTER ATTRACTIVENESS-OMETER

8.5

BECAUSE THEY ARE SO MASSIVE — AND RELATIVELY EASY TO SEE BECAUSE THEY ARE 'LOCAL'.

THE CHORUS CLAPPER HAS THE MĀORI NAME KIHIKIHI-WAWĀ. WAWĀ MEANS A ROARING SOUND LIKE HEAVY RAIN. (THE MĀORI NAMES OF FAUNA USUALLY ARE MORE DESCRIPTIVE THAN THE ENGLISH!)

WE ALL KNOW THAT CICADAS ARE LOUD. SOME SPECIES OF CICADA CAN REACH A VOLUME OF ABOUT 120 DECIBELS — ABOUT THE SAME AS AN AMBULANCE SIREN!

CRITTER ATTRACTIVENESS-OMETER
6

FOR PROVIDING THE SOUNDTRACK TO SUMMER IN AOTEAROA.

CICADAS/ KIHIKIHI/ TĀTARAKIHI

New Zealand is a pretty exciting place for cicadas — we have about 40 species, and all of them are endemic to Aotearoa. Around the world there are about 2500 species, but our 40 are found only here.

Most of the time these insects live under the soil in the nymph stage of their life cycle. After what can be several years (there's one species in America that stays underground for 17 years), they come up to the surface and make a racket to attract other cicadas so they can reproduce.

It's the males that make all the noise. Wētā, for example, make their noise by stridulating their legs, like strumming a washboard in a hillbilly band, but the cicada makes their noise through a tymbal. This 'instrument' is a membrane on the side of their abdomen. When the cicada flexes or vibrates, the tymbal pops in and out — just like when you grab a large empty soft-drink bottle and squeeze it and it does that bang-bang sound, but a cicada does it really fast — up to 600 times a second!

For early Māori, the chit-chatting of first European or English settlers was really mysterious — they couldn't understand a lot of it — so they described the chatter of the new arrivals as te reo kihikihi, or cicada language, because to their ears the sounds seemed really harsh.

The way to tell the difference between cicada species is their very distinctive songs, and that different species sing at different times of year. Clapping cicada only live in the North Island, and they start singing before Christmas. From January, you're likely to hear the delightfully named chorus clapper.

Cicadas can live in forest, rocks, scrub, tussock, grassland, riverbeds, clay banks — pretty much everywhere. A species that's part of a group known as *Maoricicada* lives in alpine zones — some as high as 1800 metres above sea level. Apart from habitat and sound, it's very difficult to figure them all out!

COOK STRAIT GIANT WĒTĀ

These fascinating insects actually live on a smattering of islands in Cook Strait, not the body of water itself. (Otherwise they really would be wetter wētā!)

Their scientific name is *Deinacrida rugosa* — deinacrida means 'terrible grasshopper', and rugosa means wrinkled. The Cook Strait giant wētā has a ridgey, more wrinkled abdomen than other giant wētā species.

They're very gentle creatures. When we think of wētā, we tend

IN OTHER SOUTHERN HEMISPHERE COUNTRIES THAT WERE ONCE PART OF GONDWANA, THEY'RE KNOWN AS KING CRICKETS.

WĒTĀ ARE MORE ANCIENT THAN OUR TUATARA. FOSSIL WĒTĀ NEARLY 200 MILLION YEARS OLD HAVE BEEN FOUND IN QUEENSLAND, FROM THE TIME WHEN WE WERE STILL CONNECTED TO AUSTRALIA.

CRITTER ATTRACTIVENESS-OMETER 8

BECAUSE THEY ARE GENTLE GIANTS THAT RESEMBLE A RHINOCEROS (IN INVERTEBRATE TERMS).

to think of the smaller ones that we see in our backyards — tree wētā — which can be pretty ferocious. But these guys are like big, trundling, harmless armoured tanks. You'd have to be really annoying a giant wētā for it to hurt you.

The Cook Strait giant wētā can't survive anywhere there are rats. There were small giant wētā populations holding out on Mana Island, Takapourewa/Stephens Island and some other islands in Cook Strait. Fortunately, some were translocated to rat-free Maud Island in the Marlborough Sounds in 1977 and to Matiu/Somes Island in Wellington Harbour in 1996. On Matiu/Somes Island, they've adapted their diet to eat the grass down. (That's better than a lawnmower!)

Some were also translocated to the Zealandia sanctuary in Wellington in 2007, after more than a century of being missing from the mainland. At one point, tiny backpack-style radio transmitters were put onto the giant wētā to figure out how much they were moving around. The males travelled nearly 300 metres, looking for females. The data also showed one giant wētā seemed to have travelled down a stream . . . except this turned out to be one that got snatched by a hungry eel (who ate the transmitter as well)!

At Zealandia there are natural predators of the Cook Strait giant wētā, including moreporks/ruru and tuatara (who particularly love them; they're like KFC for a tuatara), but in a natural ecosystem with no rats (such as predator-free islands or sanctuaries such as Zealandia), the wētā population can cope with natural predators. The sheer numbers of rats, mice, stoats, hedgehogs and other predators elsewhere mean wētā populations get hammered by an unsustainable onslaught of attackers.

Giant wētā can get pretty massive — they'll take up the entire palm of your hand. But they don't live very long. The female lays 200 or more eggs, then the young wētā hatch out and they moult and grow, moult and grow, moult and grow — until they're about two years old, when they're that enormous size, and then that's it; they're done.

CRIMSON JELLYFISH

The crimson jelly, or *Turritopsis rubra*, is a tiny little jellyfish-like critter that swarms in the shallow waters around our coasts in summer. A cool thing about the crimson jelly is that it's not a true jellyfish, it's a hydromedusa. Hydromedusae, closely related to jellyfish, are the oldest multicellular animals on the planet. They have been around for between 500 and 700 million years, so they've had a pretty good innings!

Jellies live in the ocean, as well as occasionally in freshwater lakes. The crimson jelly is a very close relative of the immortal jelly, which escapes death as an adult by reversing its life cycle! This is essentially the same as if a caterpillar turned into a butterfly then thought, 'Nah, it's getting a bit tough out here, I'll be a caterpillar again.' The immortal jelly does this when conditions are tough, and as conditions improve it can turn back into an adult. No other type of animal can do this. We don't know if the crimson jelly can also do it, but we think possibly it can, given its genetic closeness to the immortal jelly.

Don't panic if you see them — these jellies can't sting humans because their stings are too small. Crimson jellies are only a tiny 1–2 centimetres wide, about the size of a thumbnail. They are bell-shaped, and inside their clear bodies are their deep crimson-coloured organs. Their reproductive organs are the bits that you see running down the inside of the bell.

Jellyfish of this shape swim by filling up with water and then pushing it out and boosting forward.

The crimson jelly, as part of the hydromedusae family, have two stages of life: at first it's a little polyp, which is like a wee coral that sticks to stuff, almost like a tiny little anemone, then it becomes the adult medusa, which is the bit that floats around in the ocean.

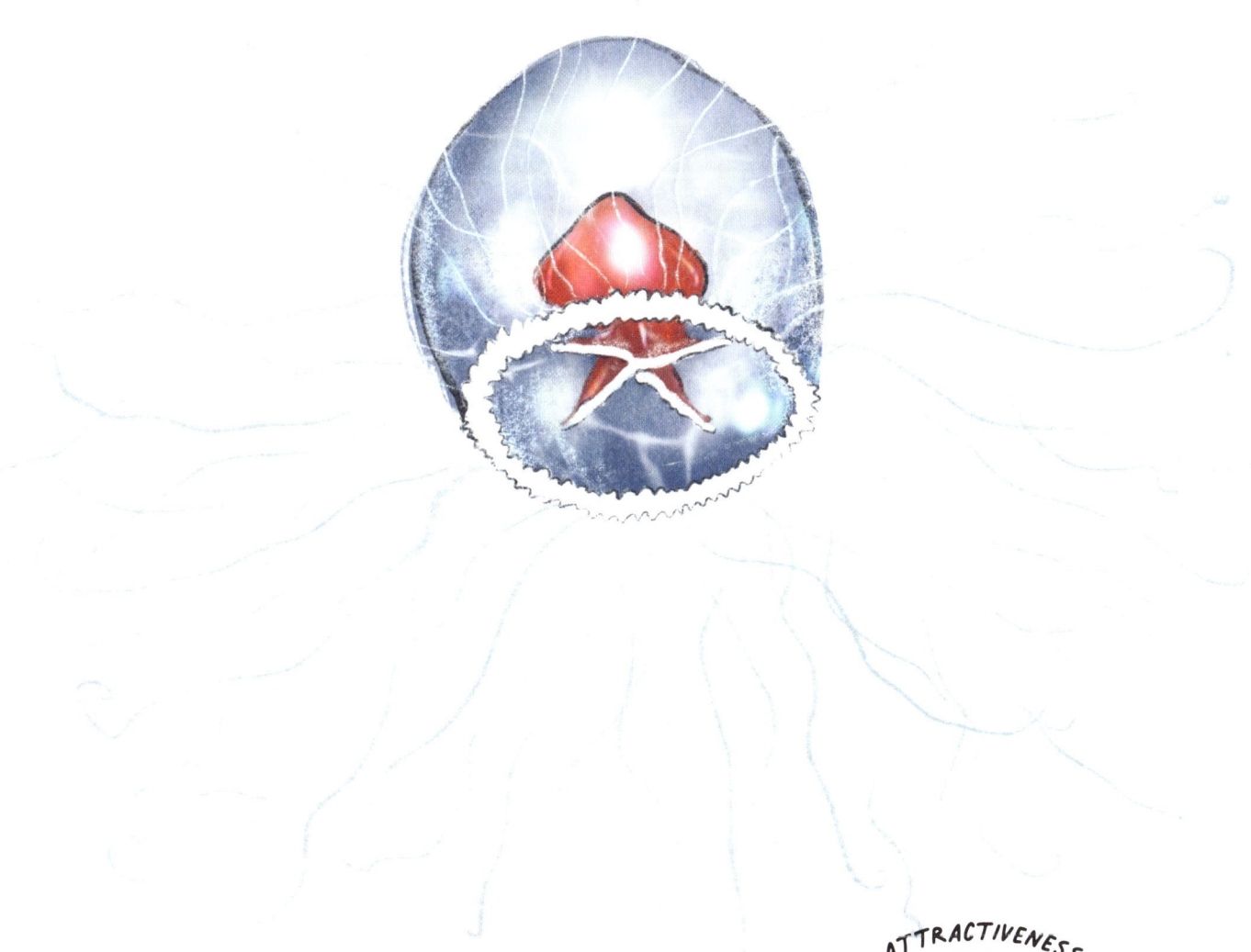

NOT ALL JELLYFISH STING, BUT THE WAY THAT JELLYFISH STINGS WORK HAS BEEN DESCRIBED AS BEING A BIT LIKE A CLUSTER BOMB. THEY RELEASE THOUSANDS OF TINY CAPSULES CALLED NEMATOCYSTS, WHICH THEN BURST OPEN AND LITTLE HARPOONS LOADED WITH VENOM DO THE STINGING! THE ANATOMY INVOLVED IN THAT KIND OF WARFARE IS INCREDIBLE!

CRITTER ATTRACTIVENESS-OMETER

9.2

FOR THEIR ETERNAL YOUTH AND THEIR GRACEFUL MODE OF TRANSPORT.

CRITTER ATTRACTIVENESS-OMETER

3

BUT ONLY BECAUSE IT IS YELLOW, AND THAT'S NIC'S FAVOURITE COLOUR.

IN EXTREME CASES, PATCHES OF DOG VOMIT SLIME MOULD CAN BE 1 METRE ACROSS AND WEIGH UP TO 20 KILOGRAMS!

IN SCANDINAVIA THEY CALL IT TROLL-CAT VOMIT; IN FINLAND, WITCHES' BUTTER.

DOG VOMIT SLIME MOULD

Sometimes called 'scrambled egg slime', *Fuligo septica* is found throughout the world and has a bunch of different common names, but in its vegetative stage it really does look like dog vomit. (Perhaps from a dog that had been eating cheese-flavoured potato chips?) If you've been out in the bush and seen a yellow, sticky, stringy, dog-vomity thing, you've probably come across it.

It's not a plant and it's not an animal; it falls somewhere in between. It's within the fungus kingdom, but what's amazing about it is that, most of the time, it exists as separate cells, doing their own thing. When it's time to reproduce, all the cells combine together like an amoeba and create this big, beautiful, yellow dog vomit. And it moves!

We don't really know that much about slime moulds in New Zealand. It's thought that we have about 160 species here; we know some are probably endemic to Aotearoa. And we know that they are easily able to move. When they're in their vegetative phase — that's the yellow dog-vomit stage, in this species — that's when they're mobile. They're actually oozing around like an amoeba, kind of engulfing everything in their path — it's quite amazing. Perhaps some of the early horror movies used the idea of this kind of slime mould as the inspiration for evil ooze or monstrous blobs.

Most of the time slime moulds are microscopic and exist as single-celled organisms, but when they all gather together and form a plasmodium in the search for food, they become highly visible to us. We know that they eat bacteria, particularly the bacteria that eats organic material, and that they play a critical role in the decomposition of organic material, so they're all part of that crucial role of cycling nutrients and creating soils.

When they come together as slime, they then form a firmer structure and that's when they reproduce. When they produce spores, as a fruiting body, they become more like a mushroom in terms of texture and shape.

They're a very, very bizarre creature. Because they don't have a clearly defined structure, in the way that most organisms that we're familiar with do, they can all just huddle in and become one giant moving thing. And when slime mould cells are congregating, they're very beautiful — you can take great photos of them!

FOREST RINGLET BUTTERFLY

The forest ringlet, also known as Helms' butterfly, used to be one of our most common lowland butterflies. It's found only here in Aotearoa, and is the only genus in its family.

Their decline is a bit of a whodunnit — we're not entirely sure what has happened to them. We do know that in recent times their numbers have dropped hugely, but we can't really point our finger at why.

Rats would probably have a crack at its larvae (caterpillars), and there is also a parasitic fly which has larvae that attack the larvae of the forest ringlet.

There's also a lot of speculation about wasps. We suspect (but don't know) that wasps have had a major impact on this species, and certainly there's some evidence that we've lost this species almost entirely from the lowland areas where it was primarily found. Now it's most often found hanging out around 700 metres above sea level, and maybe that's because wasps don't enjoy life at that altitude — it's a bit cold for them.

We think that the forest ringlet exists in the caterpillar stage for one to two years, which is quite a long time, but that the butterflies themselves are only around for about a month.

We know that it is a brush-footed butterfly species, like monarch butterflies, red admirals/kahukura and yellow admirals/kahukōwhai, and has really, really hairy forelimbs. Even though they're insects and have six legs, they don't stand on their first two. We're not entirely sure what they use these hairy legs for, but it might be for smell or communication with other butterflies.

One clear threat to a butterfly named after a forest is the loss of its habitat over time. Since humans arrived in New Zealand, our forest cover has reduced from around 80 per cent of the country to less than 23 per cent. As a result, the opportunities for a butterfly designed to thrive in forests have also declined. It means that in hotspots for this species, such as Te Kuha range on the West Coast of the South Island, protecting this forest becomes even more vital for the protection of the forest ringlet.

It's probably the cumulative impact of loss of habitat, introduced pests, climate change and parasites that are making life tough for the beautiful wee forest ringlet. European scientists have known about it since 1881, but despite that, we still don't know very much about it at all.

THE CATERPILLAR OF THE FOREST RINGLET FEEDS ON A SPECIES OF SEDGE (A LONG GRASS) CALLED GAHNIA, FOUND IN BEECH FORESTS, AND OCCASIONALLY ON SNOW TUSSOCK, WHERE YOU CAN SEE REALLY CLEAR NOTCHES MADE BY THE LARVAE.

WE KNOW THEY USED TO BE WIDESPREAD THROUGHOUT ALL OF AOTEAROA, BUT YOU'D BE LUCKY TO SEE THEM THESE DAYS. YOU MAY SEE THEM IN THE LEWIS PASS, AND YOU MIGHT SEE THEM AROUND RUAPEHU, FROM ABOUT LATE JANUARY, WHEN THEY EMERGE.

CRITTER ATTRACTIVENESS-OMETER

7.3

TROPICAL BUTTERFLIES GET ALL THE ATTENTION, BUT OUR NATIVE BUTTERFLIES ARE BEAUTIFUL AS WELL.

25

CRITTER ATTRACTIVENESS-OMETER

3

IT GOT TWO BONUS POINTS FOR LOOKING LIKE SOMETHING OUT OF STAR WARS OR DUNE.

IF YOU'RE WORRIED ABOUT THE FRESHWATER BRISTLE WORM, A GOOD WAY TO HELP PROTECT THEM IS BY PROTECTING OUR RIVERS: PLANT ALONG THE BANKS TO ADD SHADE AND STOP EROSION, AND DON'T TAKE TOO MUCH WATER FROM THEM.

NATIVE FRESHWATER BRISTLE WORMS ARE FOUND ONLY IN FOUR INLAND RIVER SYSTEMS, IN THE EASTERN NORTH ISLAND: THE TURITEA STREAM, THE TUKITUKI RIVER SYSTEM IN HAWKE'S BAY, AND THE NGARURORO AND WAIAPU RIVERS NEAR RUATORIA ON THE EAST CAPE. AND, VERY ODDLY, THEY WERE ONCE FOUND IN A CREEK IN FIJI!

FRESHWATER BRISTLE WORM

The freshwater bristle worm looks like a hideous monster you'd expect to see in a blockbuster movie, but in real life you would be lucky to see it. To take a photo of this critter you'd need a special camera, because they grow to only between 9 and 50 millimetres long. They look a little bit like a tardigrade (see pages 92–93).

There are 30,000 species of bristle worm in the world. Of those, only 168 species hang out in freshwater environments. They're also known as clam worms and rag worms around the world, and some species of them are eaten. (You'd need a big bowlful of these to get a good feed!)

This little creature has the lonely but glorious title of being Aotearoa's only freshwater bristle worm. It's important to note that while they are packaged very much like an earthworm — a cylindrical tube with segments — they're not that kind of smooth, slimy creature.

Bristle worms have no eyes. They have little bumps on their sides called parapodia (para means beyond or beside, and pod means feet, so 'beyond feet'), like fleshy bits of tentacle. They also have bristles, called chaetae, that splurge out from the parapodia and look a bit like tassels.

The most interesting thing about freshwater bristle worms, apart from their looks, is that they have these incredible teeth and mouthparts and jaws — but the teeth are not made from calcium, like human teeth, which is very unusual. Instead, they're made from a lightweight amino acid which is bound with zinc ions, making the teeth extremely tough.

Scientists are very interested in this, because if they could uncover the secrets of the worm's super-teeth, who knows what kind of amazing engineering feats we might be able to pull off by understanding that technology? Such a discovery has a lot of potential for further exploration. It may only look like a rumpty old bristle worm, but maybe it holds the key to the best new bionic limbs if your leg falls off . . . or something like that!

GIANT KNOBBLED WEEVIL

We have a wealth of weevils in Aotearoa. Scientists geek out about them because of how they've proliferated and managed to eke out an existence in such a range of places.

Hadramphus stilbocarpae — some call it stilbo for short — was first discovered on Big South Cape Island, which is one of the Tītī (Muttonbird) Islands southwest of Rakiura/Stewart Island, in 1955. Unfortunately, we think a rat plague on the islands in the 1960s wiped out the population of giant knobbled weevils there, but the good news is that they were discovered again on the islands of Fiordland and also on the Snares Islands in the subantarctic.

It is a large flightless weevil that, like many weevils, is dependent on specific host plants. This weevil particularly likes two species of plant. It was initially called the pūnui beetle after a particular kind of plant that can have leaves up to 73 centimetres across — massive. It also likes to eat one of our native carrot species. (Who knew we had a native carrot?!)

The giant knobbled weevil was one of the very first New Zealand insects to be granted legal protection under the Wildlife Act, in 1980. (It was about 40 years ago that we started to realise that we couldn't just protect the big stuff, and started to look more broadly at what was happening with our invertebrates.) It's a really special kind of creature, and another one of our amazing ancient species that has survived over thousands of years but hasn't changed their body shape very much over that period — they got onto a good design and stuck with it.

And here's just one more reason why weevils are special: we call New Zealand 'the land of birds', but there are only about 200 native bird species in Aotearoa, and we have 1500 known weevil species. Maybe we should call it Weevil Land!

THESE ARE LARGE WEEVILS! THE AVERAGE SIZE OF A WEEVIL IS 6 MILLIMETRES LONG; THIS ONE GROWS TO 25 MILLIMETRES.

THEY'RE CHARACTERS, TOO — YOU CAN ACTUALLY HEAR THEM MUNCHING ON PLANTS!

CRITTER ATTRACTIVENESS-OMETER: 6

IT'S CUTE! IF YOU MADE IT THE SIZE OF A RHINO, IT'D BE FUN TO HAVE AS A PET — KIND OF LIKE A CROSS BETWEEN AN ANKYLOSAURUS AND AN ARMOURED VEHICLE.

GLOW-IN-THE-DARK FRESHWATER SNAIL LIMPET

What a great descriptive name! The glow-in-the-dark freshwater snail limpet is, in fact, a freshwater snail limpet that glows in the dark! Although, actually, it's not *really* a limpet, but a species of snail (limpets don't generally live in freshwater). It's tiny — roughly 1 centimetre long. That's about the size of a raisin.

It makes glow-in-the-dark mucus, which is pretty amazing! The glow that they give off (bioluminescence) is the same sort of size as the glow that you get from a glow worm, but way brighter, and green.

What normally happens with bioluminescent organisms is that the chemical reaction producing light occurs internally when they're disturbed. What's interesting about the freshwater snail limpet, *Latia neratoides*, is that the bioluminescence is external. It secretes slimy, glow-in-the-dark mucus when it is disturbed, which gets expelled out into the surrounding area. If you walk through a stream full of them at night, you can end up with glowing footprints.

They're amazing little things, which can detect chemical changes in the water. If you change the chemical nature of the water — like how acidic or alkaline it is — they will also secrete the glow-in-the-dark mucus.

Like lots of snails and slugs and worms, they're hermaphrodites, which means they have both male and female parts for reproduction. Depending on who they run into, they provide the opposite equipment. About 5 per cent of all animal species are hermaphrodites, which is actually quite a good survival strategy. It's always good to be agile!

They're found in the North Island only, south of Auckland. They need well oxygenated water, much like the whio (blue duck). They're another bio-indicator of the quality of fresh water — they need a nice little forested stream with nice little stones for them to grab onto. Think of them like a miniature version of a pāua — they suck onto the stones, making them really difficult to pick off. Probably not even a whio could do it!

WE DON'T KNOW QUITE WHY THEY DRIBBLE OUT GLOW-IN-THE-DARK MUCUS, BUT IT COULD BE SOME KIND OF DEFENCE MECHANISM FOR CONFUSING OR DISTRACTING PREDATORS SO THAT THE LIMPETS CAN PROTECT THEMSELVES.

CRITTER ATTRACTIVENESS-OMETER

7–7.5

7 OR 7.5. ANYTHING THAT GLOWS IN THE DARK IS AMAZEBALLS. (JUST ASK SIOUXSIE WILES — SHE'S A BIT OF AN EXPERT ON ANYTHING GLOW-IN-THE-DARK!)

SCIENTISTS BELIEVE THE GLOW-IN-THE-DARK FRESHWATER SNAIL LIMPET IS THE WORLD'S ONLY BIOLUMINESCENT FRESHWATER ORGANISM.

31

THERE'S ACTUALLY ANOTHER TINY SNAIL NAMED AFTER GRETA, IN BRUNEI, IN SOUTHEAST ASIA, AND IT'S THE SAME SIZE. IN KENYA, THERE IS ALSO A BEETLE NAMED AFTER HER, BECAUSE ITS DISCOVERER RECKONED THAT THE ANTENNAE OF THE BEETLE RESEMBLED HER PLAITS!

SNAILS ARE ACTUALLY AMONG THE MOST THREATENED SPECIES ON EARTH. HERE IN AOTEAROA WE HAVE ABOUT 1400 SPECIES OF LAND AND FRESHWATER SNAILS AND SLUGS.

CRITTER ATTRACTIVENESS-OMETER
4

IT'S TINY, BUT MIGHTY — JUST LIKE GRETA (NOT ALL HEROES WEAR CAPES).

GRETA THUNBERG FRESHWATER SNAIL

Yes, that is this snail's actual name. Not only that, but its scientific name is *Opacuincola gretathunbergae*!

It was named for the wonderful young environmental activist Greta Thunberg in 2021. The researchers who found and named the snail wrote a beautiful dedication to her, saying that they chose the name in her honour. By starting with a single-person school strike, which led to world-wide demonstrations (primarily by young people) to save our climate, Greta managed to finally get momentum in global politics towards action on climate change.

This particular freshwater snail is pretty special because, apart from ticking all of our critter boxes, it is less than 3 millimetres long! That's smaller than a grain of rice!

We have about 70 species of freshwater snail in New Zealand, and this particular genus has around 25 species. Of those, four species are in the nationally critical pack, one is naturally uncommon, and all the rest are categorised as 'data deficient'. The Greta Thunberg snail is one of the data-deficient ones, meaning we simply don't know enough about them to be able to protect them.

The Greta Thunberg freshwater snail is a true crenobiont, meaning an organism found in springs and brooks. This beautiful little snail's range is limited to a tiny trickle on the side of a road in the Cobb Valley in Kahurangi National Park. That's poignant, because if it's limited to a trickle, and climate change is impacting on that trickle's existence, then we may lose this snail as well. Being named Greta Thunberg puts a lot of responsibility on this snail — there's so much about this little creature that represents bigger issues.

The Greta Thunberg snail eats organic slimes. It grazes on bacterial, fungal and algal films and bits of decaying stuff. (Someone's got to eat the gross stuff!)

Its shell has three-and-a-half whorls (spirals) and has a beautiful marbled appearance. Its other defining feature is an orange operculum on its shell, which is like a trapdoor. When conditions start to get dry, it can flip this little trapdoor shut so it can retain moisture inside its shell.

Scientists had been trying to warn us about climate change for more than 30 years, but had been ignored. Greta managed to grab people by the heartstrings and move them towards action. It seems very appropriate that this snail should be named after her.

CRITTER ATTRACTIVENESS-OMETER

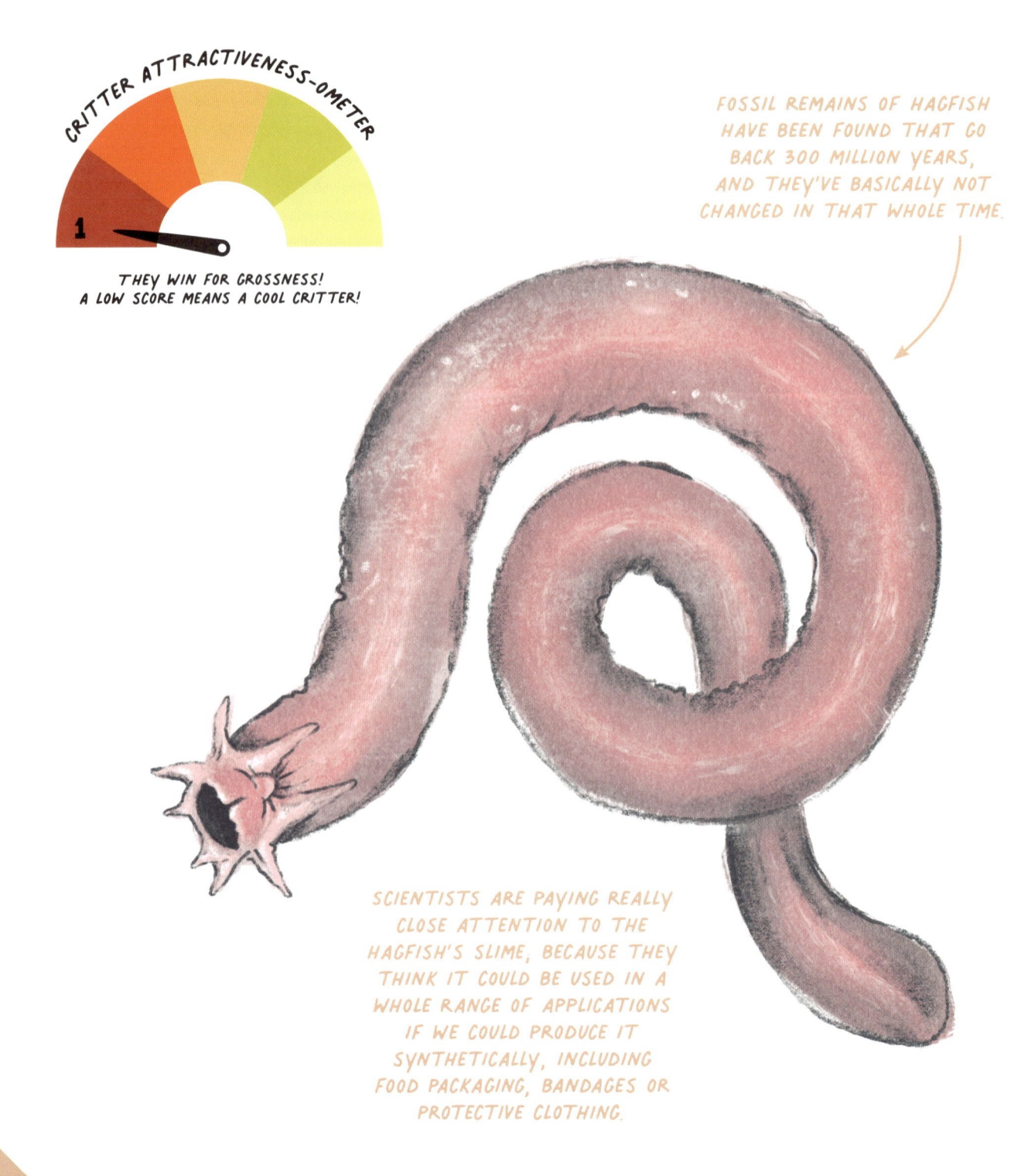

1

THEY WIN FOR GROSSNESS!
A LOW SCORE MEANS A COOL CRITTER!

FOSSIL REMAINS OF HAGFISH HAVE BEEN FOUND THAT GO BACK 300 MILLION YEARS, AND THEY'VE BASICALLY NOT CHANGED IN THAT WHOLE TIME.

SCIENTISTS ARE PAYING REALLY CLOSE ATTENTION TO THE HAGFISH'S SLIME, BECAUSE THEY THINK IT COULD BE USED IN A WHOLE RANGE OF APPLICATIONS IF WE COULD PRODUCE IT SYNTHETICALLY, INCLUDING FOOD PACKAGING, BANDAGES OR PROTECTIVE CLOTHING.

HAGFISH

Hagfish are a very old species of jawless fish related to the lamprey. They're found all over the world, but we have about eight species in Aotearoa. They may look repulsive, but they're vitally important.

If you annoy them, they produce this strange, gelatinous slime in self-defence. And if you put them in a bucket of water, within seconds, the water turns into what can only be described as a bucket of snot!

Hagfish have a number of glands along their body that hold all the little filaments that create the slime. These filaments are a hundred times thinner than human hair but ten times stronger than nylon! It's another one of those incredible examples where nature totally has us beat when it comes to that kind of technical design.

Hagfish are seldom seen by humans as they are generally found at the bottom of the ocean. They're blind, but they have little tentacles around the front of their mouths.

They have a crucial role in the ocean ecosystem, which is to clean up carrion. They eat dead whales and fish and other stuff that falls to the ocean floor. In order to do this, they essentially tie their tail in a knot, creating a sort of spring effect, which gives them enough power to smash their faces into the dead flesh of these animals! They play such a vital role by getting rid of dead bodies and helping cycle those nutrients back through the marine ecosystem.

Hagfish have two rows of scary-looking teeth on each side of their mouth, which look like a circular saw attached to their head. They're sort of eel-shaped and, depending on the species, can grow up to half a metre long.

Why aren't bigger fish very successful in attacking them? That comes down to the slime. It's created by a really complex chemical reaction involving a whole lot of interconnected proteins and polymers, essentially bundled up like little skeins of wool inside. When the reaction happens, these shoot out of the glands on the sides of the hagfish and basically just sludge up the water until it's almost impenetrable. And that's their defence. You can't get your mouth around a hagfish if you've just had a faceful of slime!

HARLEQUIN GECKO

The harlequin gecko is probably the most stunning of all of our reptiles. It looks like something out of *Game of Thrones*.

Harlequin geckos are fascinating animals. Their scientific name is *Tukutuku rakiurae*. The name tukutuku makes perfect sense, because if you've ever been onto a marae and seen the woven panels between the posts of the meeting house, they are called tukutuku panels, and the chevron-looking pattern looks like what you see on the harlequin gecko. They live on Stewart Island, the Māori name for which is Rakiura — hence the second part of their scientific name.

They're also cool because of their physiology: they're one of the most southern-living geckos on the planet. They live in the Roaring Forties — below 40 degrees of latitude — where it rains about 1600 millimetres a year (which is a lot!) and gets down to about −10 degrees Celsius, so they are very much tough Southerners!

Because they are so enigmatic and live somewhere so remote, it can be very hard to get an idea of how they're doing as a population. We haven't quite managed to get rid of introduced predators on Rakiura/Stewart Island yet, so all three types of rat we have in Aotearoa, and feral cats, are probably a problem for them.

Reptiles can be easy pickings for rodent pests. They're ectothermic ('cold-blooded'), so they rely on the surrounding temperature to generate energy to move. If the temperature is at 0 degrees for a week, which it can be down there, then they're not going to be able to run away from any predators, and will be a nice little protein package for any rats that come across them.

They generally give birth to twins. Due to living in such extreme cold temperatures, harlequin geckos are pregnant for at least 24 months (that's two years!). To give that some perspective, Komodo dragons (which are much bigger reptiles) are only pregnant for about eight months.

They're on our threatened list; currently they are listed as nationally endangered. It's a combination of being at risk from predators and scientists just not being able to find enough of them to draw a big enough conclusion.

LIKE MOST GECKOS, THEY LIKE TO EAT INSECTS BUT WILL ALSO EAT SMALL FRUITS.

HARLEQUIN GECKOS ARE NOCTURNAL.

CRITTER ATTRACTIVENESS-OMETER

9

THEY LOOK LIKE THEY'VE BEEN PAINTED BY AN ARTIST — STUNNING.

HELMS' STAG BEETLE

We have about 40 species of stag beetle in Aotearoa; Helms' is our largest one. It grows to 4.5 centimetres long if it's a bloke beetle.

They're named 'stag beetles' because the males have these big 'antlers' that they use for sniffing along the ground, but also for picking each other up and flipping each other over — they're the judo masters of the beetle world. The antlers are part of their jaws, and they do look like the antlers on a stag.

To carry the weight of their huge antlers, they have massive upper bodies. They kind of look like bodybuilders who are doing all upper body and no legs!

Helms' stag beetles are generally found in and under the forest litter, and are active at night. They're found from Karamea on the West Coast to the south of the South Island, across to Tapanui in Otago.

They're interesting because they can live from the coast right up to the alpine zone, which suggests a very flexible ecological approach to life, which is probably why they're still trucking along. They can live in forest- and tussock-dominated high country, right down to islands and coastal areas.

They're largely found in places like Whenua Hou/Codfish Island and Rakiura/Stewart Island. We don't quite know what they're eating, but beetles have been seen at night feeding on the sap of trees, kahikatea in particular. While they may stay in their larval stage for a long time, the adult beetles probably only live for several weeks, during which time they are probably looking for high-energy food so that they can go out and find a partner and make some beetle kids.

These stag beetles are very big, but they don't fly (a recurring theme for New Zealand wildlife!), which makes them really vulnerable to being eaten by rats, mice and also pigs. Not a fun fact — but a pretty fascinating one — is that Helms' stag beetles have been found to make up more than a quarter of what's found inside the stomachs of feral pigs!

As our climate changes, the range of invertebrate fauna such as the stag beetle is probably going to become more restricted, making species like this even more threatened. It's an offence under the Wildlife Act to hunt or kill or even have a Helms' stag beetle, so it's best to leave it alone if you find one. Just let it get on with its very slow but very grunty approach to the world.

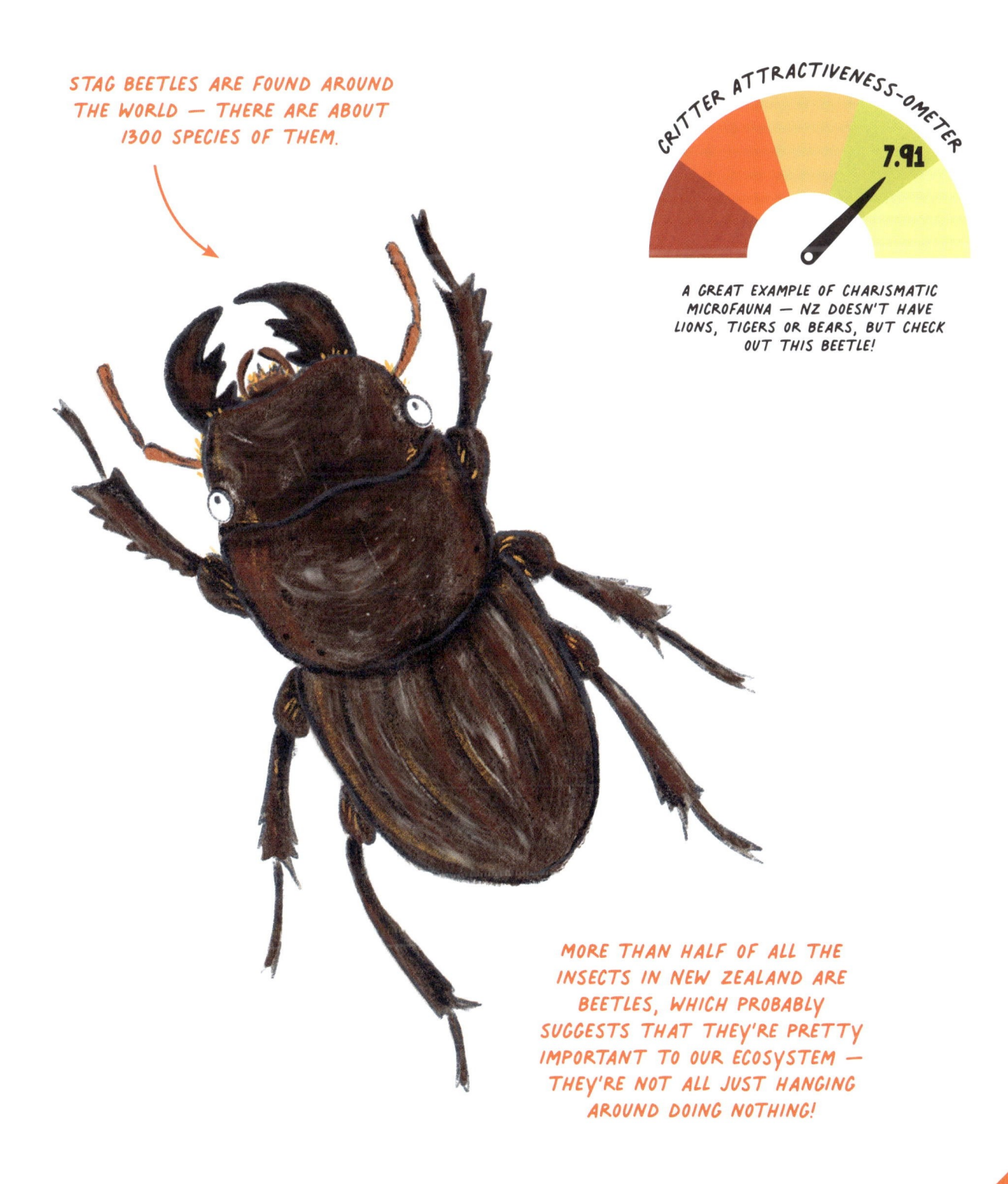

STAG BEETLES ARE FOUND AROUND THE WORLD — THERE ARE ABOUT 1300 SPECIES OF THEM.

CRITTER ATTRACTIVENESS-OMETER

7.91

A GREAT EXAMPLE OF CHARISMATIC MICROFAUNA — NZ DOESN'T HAVE LIONS, TIGERS OR BEARS, BUT CHECK OUT THIS BEETLE!

MORE THAN HALF OF ALL THE INSECTS IN NEW ZEALAND ARE BEETLES, WHICH PROBABLY SUGGESTS THAT THEY'RE PRETTY IMPORTANT TO OUR ECOSYSTEM — THEY'RE NOT ALL JUST HANGING AROUND DOING NOTHING!

CRITTER ATTRACTIVENESS-OMETER

6

NOT ONLY BECAUSE OF THEIR AWESOME SPIKY NATURE BUT ALSO BECAUSE OF THE BRIGHT HIGHLIGHTER-PINK UNDERNEATH THEIR FORELEGS.

OUR ONES ARE HARMLESS — YOU CAN PICK THEM UP AND HAVE A WEE LOOK AT THEM IF YOU DO IT VERY GENTLY — BUT IN AMERICA THERE'S ONE THAT APPEARS TO STAND UP AND RAISE ITS FORELEGS AND SPRAYS SOME CHEMICAL THAT CAN BLIND YOU!

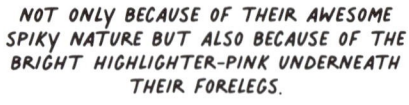

OVER TIME, WINGS HAVE EVOLVED SEPARATELY FOUR DIFFERENT TIMES FOR STICK INSECTS: THEY STARTED WITH NO WINGS, THEN THEY EVOLVED THEM, THEN THEY LOST THEM, THEN THEY EVOLVED THEM AGAIN, THEN THEY LOST THEM AGAIN!

HORRID STICK INSECT

Horrid isn't just an adjective that we've added to its name; it's its actual name! *Argosarchus horridus* is its scientific name — horridus means bristly in Latin.

We're lucky to have stick insects in Aotearoa, because they're more known as a tropical species, so how they've managed to survive the cool temperatures and glacial periods that we've had across this country remains a mystery.

They're part of the order Phasmatodea (phasm means phantom; that's because you spot one, then it disappears again). There are around 3000 phasmid species across the world.

They're very hard to see even when you're staring right at them and you know they're there. They're generally only active at night.

All our endemic species have no wings. Some species elsewhere in the world have wings, but very few of them actually fly. And of the species that can fly, only the males actually do.

They don't have ears either, and they can't make a sound, but they obviously can see or feel what's going on around them, because they'll sometimes move away if you try to pick them up.

What do they do if they sense an enemy coming a bit too close? They can sway in the wind, channelling their inner twig ('Don't look at me; I'm just a stick!'), or they may drop onto the ground, lying perfectly still. Not great tactics if you're being chased by something, and they probably get eaten by rats and possums — we don't see as many in our backyards as we used to or would expect to. Or maybe we're just not looking closely enough!

They can grow up to 20 centimetres long, which is pretty large, but there's one in Malaysia that can grow up to 35 centimetres, and another in New Guinea that's as thick as your finger and called a policeman's truncheon.

Horrid stick insect females can mate with males if they want to, or they can just reproduce female clones using the cells they have inside them. They browse on native plants, mostly, like lacebark or ribbonwood, but they eat all sorts of other native plants. They also really like the leaves of roses, raspberries and blackberries.

HUHU

Everyone knows about huhu beetles, and perhaps you might even have eaten a huhu grub. Their scientific name is *Prionoplus reticularis*, and there are a number of Māori names for the grub, including tunga haere. However, both beetles and grubs are commonly referred to as huhu. Huhu beetles are everywhere around Aotearoa — they live from coastal areas right up to 1400 metres above sea level — and we notice them because they're so large.

They live as larvae (the grubs) for about three years, and then they hatch out as adults, which only live for two weeks. Summer nights are when we start to see the adults bumbling around. They're a bit clumsy and they crash into things. They look like a little Hercules aircraft, and due to their size, it can take them up to half an hour to get airborne.

They have massively long antennae. They're sometimes known as haircutter bugs, because once you get a huhu beetle in your hair, it sometimes panics, flails around and ties itself in knots, and in the end the only thing you can do is cut your hair to get it out! To Māori, the grubs were a very important food source, and they just ate them raw. But eating the beetles could be dangerous — there's a story that a huhu beetle was pounced on and eaten by a cat, and the following morning the cat was crook and by the next afternoon it was dead! So it wouldn't pay to eat the adult huhu beetle.

Magpies particularly like to eat the beetles — they get up really early in the morning and snap up straggler huhu who haven't quite made it home yet. And moreporks often sit around outdoor lights to catch huhu.

Huhu feed on rotting wood in the forest — they're essentially part of nature's enormous waste-disposal army. They chew the wood, digest it and excrete it into tiny little pieces of wood fibre, which becomes part of the soil and food for other bugs. They're essentially driving ecosystems, the way that many invertebrates do.

Is the major threat to them habitat loss? Yes, but also they need lots of wood for the larvae to chew away on, and the grubs are pretty fussy: the moisture content of the wood has to be at least 25 per cent. If you're a grub that spends the vast majority of your life sitting in a rotten log chewing up wood but you can only chew wood that's 25 per cent moist . . . what happens over time in terms of climate change? And what happens to the function of that ecosystem if we can't process the wood as effectively as huhu do? Yet another reason for us all to go out and make good choices to help reduce our climate change impacts.

THEY CAN BITE, SO IT PAYS NOT TO ANNOY THEM. BUT THEY'RE PRETTY DOCILE, SO IF YOU DO FIND ONE THAT HAS ACCIDENTALLY STUMBLED INTO YOUR LOUNGE, JUST GENTLY PICK IT UP AND POP IT BACK OUTSIDE.

CRITTER ATTRACTIVENESS-OMETER

GRUB: 3 / BEETLE: 6
(BECAUSE IT LOOKS LIKE A LANDCRUISER.)

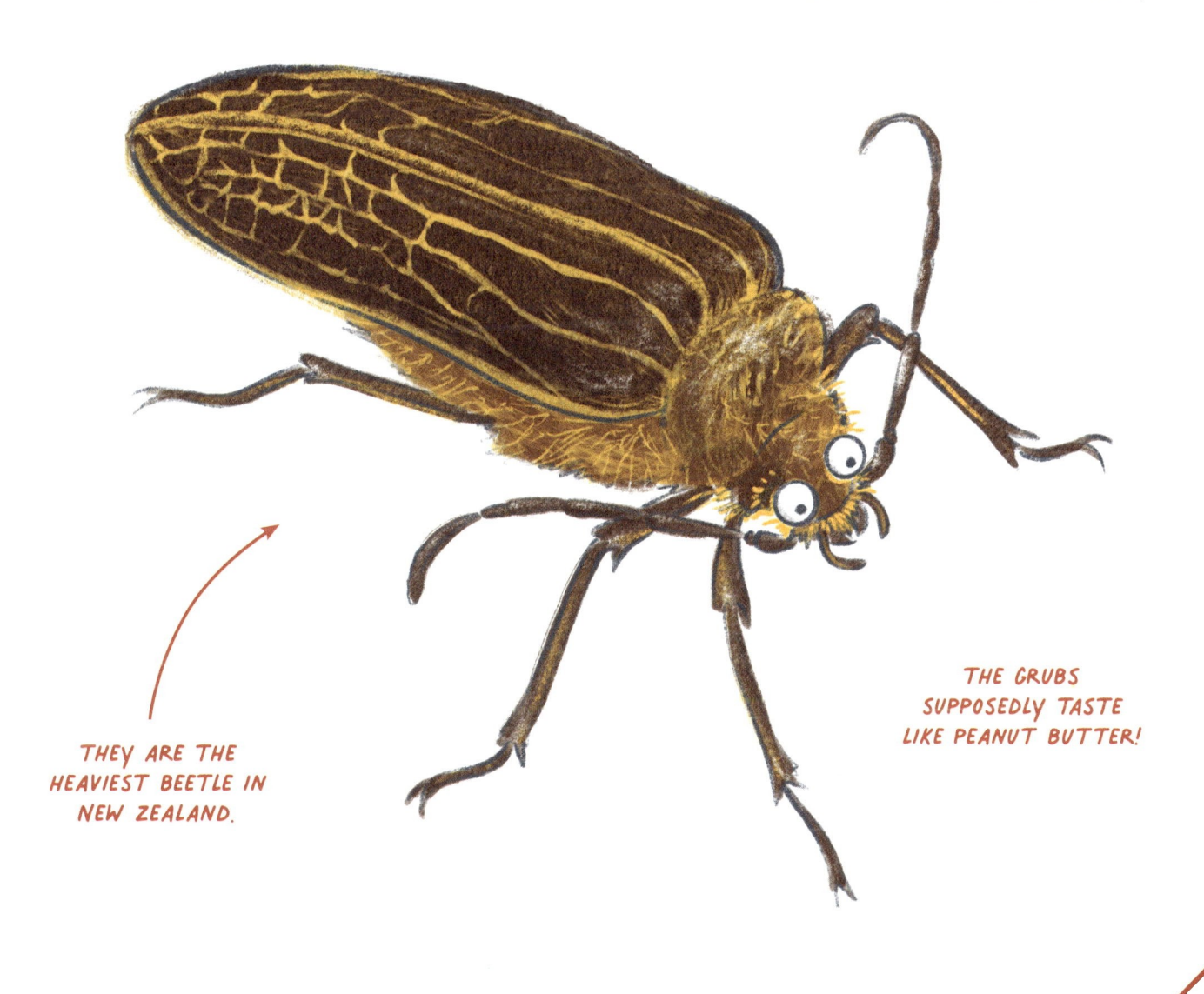

THEY ARE THE HEAVIEST BEETLE IN NEW ZEALAND.

THE GRUBS SUPPOSEDLY TASTE LIKE PEANUT BUTTER!

KATIPŌ SPIDER

The katipō is infamous in New Zealand because it's essentially the only thing on land that's poisonous and might do you some damage (unlike in Australia, where, it appears, everything is poisonous!).

Katipō means 'night stinger' in Māori, so obviously they knew about that bite! But are bites from them really that dangerous? The answer is no. The last time anyone was recorded as dying after being bitten by one was in 1901 and, before that, a couple of young children in the 1840s (and there may have also partly been an allergic reaction).

Katipō are from the black widow group of spiders

KATIPŌ FRIGHTEN PEOPLE, BUT IT SHOULD PROBABLY BE THE OTHER WAY AROUND — KATIPŌ SHOULD BE MORE SCARED OF US THAN WE ARE OF THEM.

THEY WON'T ATTACK YOU UNLESS YOU ACCIDENTALLY SIT ON THEM, SO LOOK OUT BEFORE YOU SETTLE DOWN ON THE BEACH.

CRITTER ATTRACTIVENESS-OMETER: 7.5

FOR THEIR BEAUTIFUL BRIGHT COLOUR.

and their venom can certainly do you some damage. The female's venom is more potent, and the males are thought to be too small to bite humans.

They're part of a group known as comb-footed spiders, who spin haphazard-looking webs to trip insects stumbling through them and snare them, hang them up off the ground, then wrap them up to be eaten later. Unlike other black widow spiders, the katipō female doesn't eat the male.

Their first defence mechanism is just to curl up into a ball and drop to the ground. Its other defence mechanism is to spit out silk.

North Island katipō don't have that distinctive red marking on the back; and generally neither do the males, which are smaller and white with black stripe patterns. Scientists once thought the North Island and South Island katipō were different species, but now it's thought they're the same species, just with different colours.

The katipō is a coastal spider and is found in sand dunes. It's a really specialised habitat. They like to hang out under native vegetation such as pīngao (or pīkao). Introduced vegetation such as marram grass and lupins can take over their habitat and force them to move elsewhere. That's the main threat to katipō — that and people driving their four-wheel-drives on the beach.

Another threat to katipō is its introduced relatives. Redbacks have been here since about the 1970s. Probably more threatening is a South African version, called *Steatoda*. It breeds more quickly, so when a natural event like a flood or king tide occurs, *Steatoda* populations can come back quite quickly, whereas katipō find it really hard to recover.

Katipō are now protected under the New Zealand Wildlife Act, so if you were to kill one on purpose, you could end up in jail or with a $100,000 fine. It is one of the few invertebrates that is protected under the Act, along with giant wētā, the giant knobbled weevil and a couple of others.

Even though katipō are endangered, there is hope. In coastal places where introduced weeds have been controlled, katipō numbers are actually increasing. So it's a good news story, and it's a real easy fix: do some weeding, and don't drive on the beach!

THE FEMALE KUPE'S GRASS MOTH DOESN'T FLY; THE MALES CAN SORT OF FLY BUT NOT VERY WELL. THE MALES' WINGSPAN IS ABOUT 15 MILLIMETRES, AND THE FEMALE JUST HAS WEE STUMPY WINGS.

CRITTER ATTRACTIVENESS-OMETER

4

BECAUSE IT HAS SOME CAMOUFLAGE ABILITIES AND BECAUSE ITS EYES LOOK LIKE SOMEONE STUCK A TIGER'S EYEBALL ON A MOTH!

FEMALES WEREN'T EVEN FOUND BY SCIENTISTS UNTIL 2012 — AND THAT WAS WITH PEOPLE ACTIVELY GOING OUT HUNTING FOR THEM OVER A VERY LONG TIME.

KUPE'S GRASS MOTH

Kupea electilis, or Kupe's grass moth, is a mysterious, subterranean grass moth. They are from the family Crambidae, and that means that they're a snout moth — they have quite a long snout. And they're the only species in the genus of *Kupea*, named after Kupe, the first Polynesian explorer of Aotearoa, so it's a big name for a wee moth!

They live only on Kaitōrete Spit — the long finger of land that divides Lake Ellesmere or Te Waihora from the sea, an incredible place of natural and cultural history. It's a dryland ecosystem, thriving with all manner of species like katipō and geckos and moths and wonderful plants. It's a huge place dotted with archaeological treasures, because Te Waihora was really like a supermarket for Māori, full of flounder and eels and other foods. Kaitōrete is a very special place, in particular to local rūnaka (rūnanga) of Ngāi Tahu.

The moths are pretty dusty looking and scruffy — they're those kind of moths that look like they would crumble if you touched them — but they do have striking yellow eyes. Kupe's grass moth lives under the ground on the roots of the prickly couch grass which grows in the sand dunes and gravel.

The moth is considered nationally vulnerable. The challenge for them is that people like to get in their four-wheel-drives or on their motorbikes and do doughnuts in the sand dunes. Rabbits are another pest that they need to be protected from.

There are only four colonies of Kupe's grass moths that we know about, and these are actively monitored. In 2018, the last survey, only 24 males were found. If this happened with kākāpō, it'd be on the front page of all the newspapers — but because they're grass moths, it just sort of slides under the radar.

Given its cultural importance and significance to local iwi, DOC works very closely with Ngāi Tahu to try to find the best way to protect these sites. But it is a real challenge when you're a species that has evolved to live on a tiny little plant on a tiny little piece of New Zealand and nowhere else. It needs all the love it can get!

LEAF-VEINED SLUG

It's hard to be enamoured of slugs. Why is that — is it the texture? But if you were going to rate slugs, these native ones would be way more interesting than the introduced ones we're used to seeing.

In this case, the name almost says it all. The leaf-veined slug looks like a leaf. They can be really big — some could sit quite comfortably in the palm of your hand (if you were comfortable with that). They can be all different colours. And one was discovered a few years ago that could puff up its spiky back.

The leaf-veined slug is a bit unusual. All slugs are snails that have evolved to lose their shells, and in some species you can see where it was. But the leaf-veined slug, like all of our wildlife in Aotearoa, is really ancient. They're so old that there's no way you can tell where the shell would have been. Think of it as a dinosaur of the mollusc world.

Leaf-veined slugs probably hark back to Gondwana days, because similar species are found in the other broken-off bits of this ancient supercontinent like Vanuatu, New Caledonia and Australia. So we know that they are very, very old as a species.

There are about 30 species of native slugs all over Aotearoa, part of about 1400 species of terrestrial molluscs (including slugs, snails and micro-snails) here.

Some leaf-veined slugs are endangered, and that's to do with loss of their habitat. They want nice big, earthy patches of native bush to live in. They are also eaten by rats and mice and pigs — all the usual suspects.

CRITTER ATTRACTIVENESS-OMETER

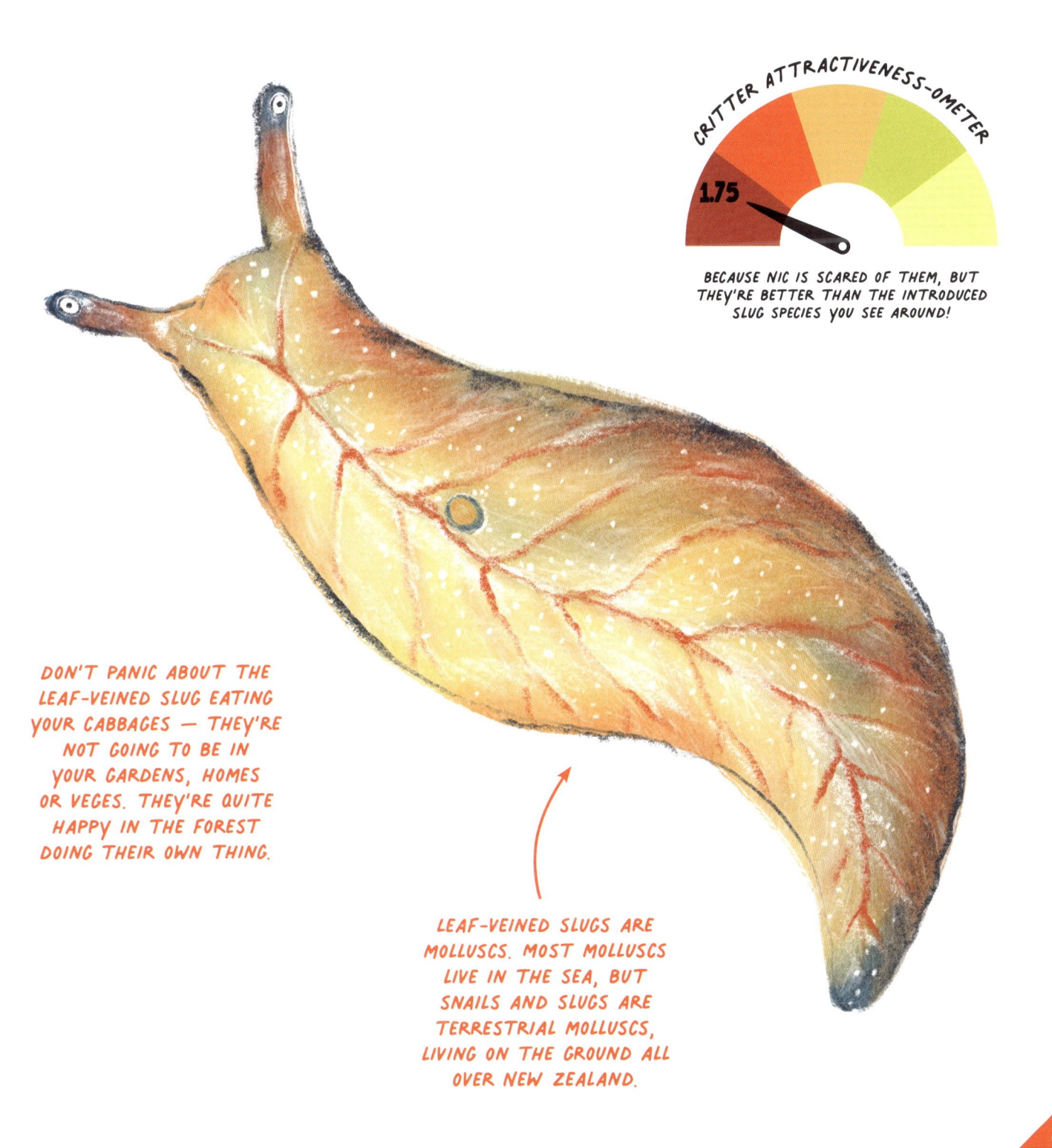

1.75

BECAUSE NIC IS SCARED OF THEM, BUT THEY'RE BETTER THAN THE INTRODUCED SLUG SPECIES YOU SEE AROUND!

DON'T PANIC ABOUT THE LEAF-VEINED SLUG EATING YOUR CABBAGES — THEY'RE NOT GOING TO BE IN YOUR GARDENS, HOMES OR VEGES. THEY'RE QUITE HAPPY IN THE FOREST DOING THEIR OWN THING.

LEAF-VEINED SLUGS ARE MOLLUSCS. MOST MOLLUSCS LIVE IN THE SEA, BUT SNAILS AND SLUGS ARE TERRESTRIAL MOLLUSCS, LIVING ON THE GROUND ALL OVER NEW ZEALAND.

LONG-TAILED BAT

BATS ARE NEW ZEALAND'S ONLY NATIVE LAND MAMMALS, AND ARE KNOWN TO MĀORI AS PEKAPEKA.

There were, at one time (up until 1967), three types of bat in Aotearoa, but there are now only two: short- and long-tailed. Long-tailed bats probably flew over from Australia a million or so years ago and have been here ever since. They were once so common that they were found under bridges on the Avon River in Christchurch until the late 1880s.

Long-tailed bats are smaller than short-tailed bats (which, in terms of their body length, are just longer than the length of your thumb, with a 15–20-centimetre wingspan). Despite their small size, they can fly at 60 kilometres per hour and 20 kilometres at a time.

THE THIRD SPECIES OF NATIVE BAT, NOW EXTINCT, WAS THE GREATER SHORT-TAILED BAT, WHICH WAS ONCE FOUND ALL OVER NEW ZEALAND. THE LAST OF ITS KIND LIVED ON REMOTE ISLANDS OFF RAKIURA / STEWART ISLAND BUT WERE ERADICATED BY RATS.

CRITTER ATTRACTIVENESS-OMETER

7.8

BECAUSE NIC LOVES THEM (IF SHE COULD HAVE A PET ONE, SHE WOULD).

Long-tailed bats roost in colonies in old, hollowed-out trees, and they move between roost trees regularly. Why? Nobody really knows! They'll hang out in one roost tree for a little bit, then everyone'll just pack up and shift. And if you're a mother bat (who weighs a grand total of only about 13 grams), that means carrying your baby (weighing maybe 7 grams), so they're pretty tough for such a wee creature.

Long-tailed bats are called long-tails because if you stretch them out, they have a membrane that attaches to their wings and goes right to the bottom of their long tail. They use that as a plate to feed off — they catch insects in mid-air and then eat them off that membrane.

They echo-locate — using sonar to find things — and they can detect something as small as a sandfly in pitch darkness. Bats are considered to be a natural insecticide — in the United States, scientists calculated that the loss of bats in agricultural areas might cost up to half a billion dollars a year in lost crops, because bats are so important for keeping insect numbers down.

In some places in New Zealand bats are making a comeback, such as Hamilton and the Waitākere Ranges in Auckland (council staff there run 'bat walks' for the public to see them). Geraldine in the South Island has one of the last remaining populations on the east coast of the South Island, where the community has embraced the long-tailed bat and done a lot to help them, including protecting important roost trees on private property that might have otherwise become firewood.

So hang on to those dead old trees, especially if they've got holes in them, because they could become perfect sites for bats to live in. These bats are pretty adaptable — they can even roost in willow trees or other non-native trees — they just need the right habitat.

To thrive, bats need quite a lot of pest control. There have been many 1080 operations over the years in Fiordland which have seen bat numbers go up significantly, because, as you can imagine, if you nest in a hollow tree and a rat or a possum or a stoat gets in, it's all over.

CRITTER ATTRACTIVENESS-OMETER

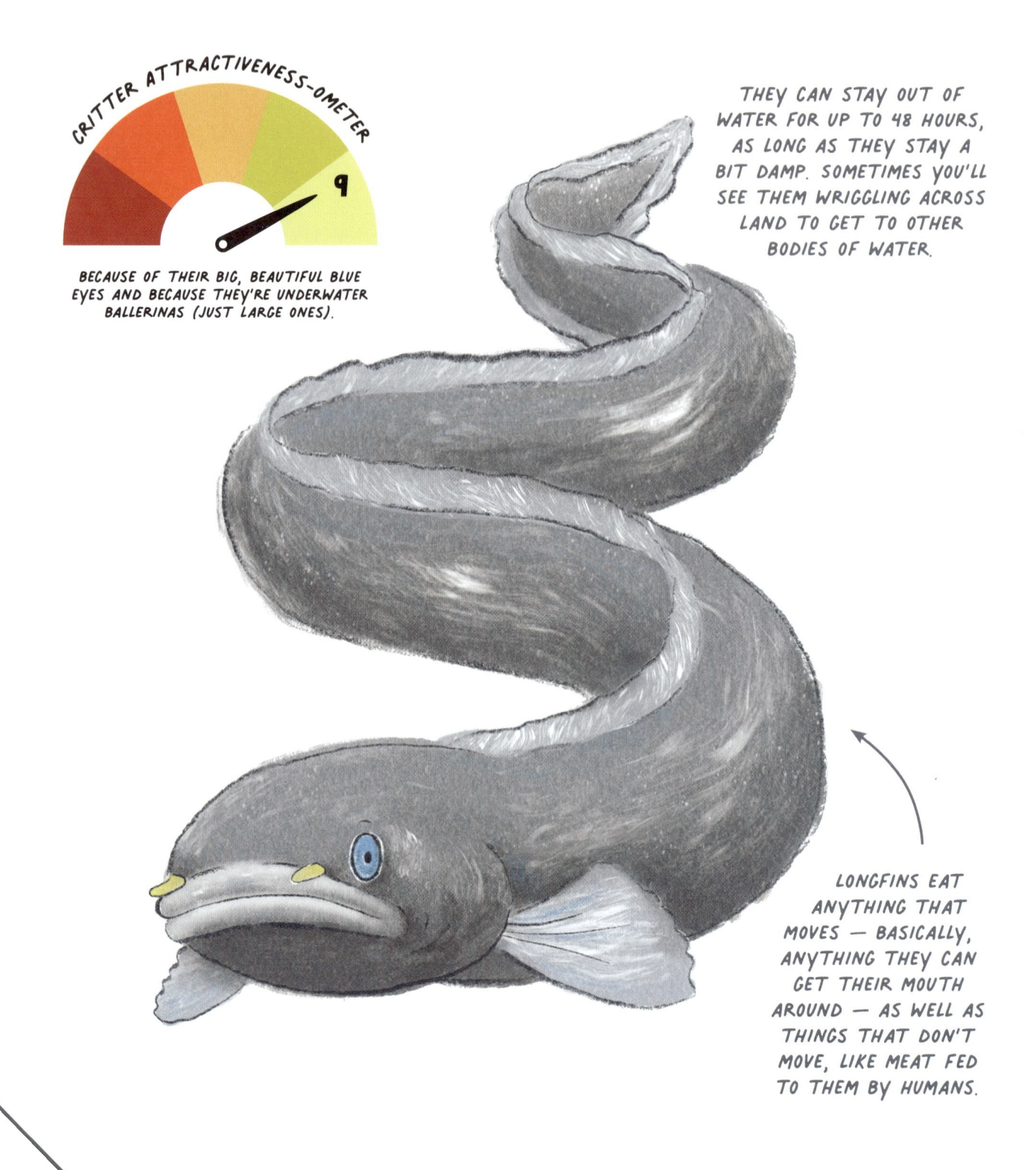

9

BECAUSE OF THEIR BIG, BEAUTIFUL BLUE EYES AND BECAUSE THEY'RE UNDERWATER BALLERINAS (JUST LARGE ONES).

THEY CAN STAY OUT OF WATER FOR UP TO 48 HOURS, AS LONG AS THEY STAY A BIT DAMP. SOMETIMES YOU'LL SEE THEM WRIGGLING ACROSS LAND TO GET TO OTHER BODIES OF WATER.

LONGFINS EAT ANYTHING THAT MOVES — BASICALLY, ANYTHING THEY CAN GET THEIR MOUTH AROUND — AS WELL AS THINGS THAT DON'T MOVE, LIKE MEAT FED TO THEM BY HUMANS.

LONGFIN EEL / TUNA

Longfin eels are beautiful (Nic always wants to cuddle them!), and they have an incredible life history. To Māori, they're taonga and sometimes taniwha.

Longfin eels are the largest freshwater eel in the world, and they're also the most ancient — this species has been around at least 80 million years. Once upon a time, they could weigh up to 40 kilograms! One of their key adaptations are their horn-like nostrils for detecting prey in the water.

None of the eels in Aotearoa mate here. They sit in our waterways in their little territories — which could be as far as 350 kilometres up a river from the sea — and grow for up to 80 years. Then they head off out to sea and swim thousands of kilometres to some mysterious place in the Pacific (possibly off Tonga or Vanuatu — we're not sure yet), where they meet up with many other eels and have an intense mating session and then die. Finally, their tiny little leaf-like larvae somehow make their way back here, and the cycle starts again.

The key part of their life cycle is that they only reproduce once. So any eel you take out of the system is an eel that's never going to breed. And perhaps that's where we've gone a bit wrong with eels: as kids, lots of us went eeling, and they are also fished commercially. These beautiful things are now in gradual decline.

The way to tell longfin and shortfin eel species apart is simple. Both eels have a fin on the top and the bottom, but the longfin's top fin is quite a bit longer than its bottom fin and comes closer to its head, whereas the shortfin's top and bottom fins are similar in length and start further down the body. And often longfin eels are bigger.

So what threatens them, in addition to fishing by humans? Water pollution and destruction of waterways. Eels need a variety of habitats, including little ripply patches of fast-flowing water over a stony bottom — that's where they catch their food — and big, deep pools for resting in.

Longfin eels are so important to our waterways because they're apex predators. If you think of them like a tiger or a lion, that's the way to picture how they fit into that ecosystem, at the top of the food chain. If they are doing well, it means there are healthy populations of their prey, which are there due to a healthy habitat, all of which makes up the ecosystem. So eels are a great indicator of a healthy waterway.

MANTIS SHRIMP

Like the tadpole shrimp (see pages 90–91), the mantis shrimp (*Heterosquilla tricarinata*) is not actually a shrimp at all. In fact, mantis shrimps belong to a group of animals called stomatopods — carnivorous marine crustaceans that go back 340 million years, well beyond dinosaurs, well beyond tuatara. And they basically haven't changed in that time. Mantis shrimps are also one of the most sophisticated marine predators on the planet, despite being only 75–100 millimetres long.

There are eight mantis shrimp species endemic to New Zealand, and two different kinds: either 'smashers' or 'spearers'. They have very fierce-looking front legs (this is also probably where the 'mantis' comes from, because they look a little bit like a praying mantis), which they fold up and then shoot them out at ridiculous speeds in order to either smash their prey or spear it!

Spearing shrimps, like the one we're talking about here, basically stab their food and then eat it like a kebab off the end of its spear, which it then folds up like a Swiss army knife, back into itself. The spear strike of a mantis shrimp moves at 35 kilometres an hour and is all over in 8 milliseconds — you'd never see it coming.

Conversely, a smasher's punch is 50 times faster than a blink of an eye, and can reach speeds of 80 kilometres an hour from a standing start. The comparative pain involved in being the victim of the smashing mantis's punch is the equivalent of dropping 20 bowling balls onto your palm! In California, a mantis shrimp shattered the safety glass of the aquarium it was in!

Mantis shrimps have eyes that move independently, and their eyesight has been described as the most sophisticated vision of any predator species on earth. For comparison, the kārearea (New Zealand falcon) has eight times greater visual acuity than a human (meaning the ability of the eye to distinguish shapes and the details of objects), because when you're a predator you need to see stuff to catch it. Humans have three types of photoreceptors in their eyes; mantis shrimp eyes have between 12 and 16 types of photoreceptors. (Maybe they can see the future!) A mantis shrimp can detect light we cannot see and can apparently even detect cancerous tumours!

You couldn't make this creature up in terms of its survivability, or its ferocity, which has remained unchanged for 340 million years.

THEY CAN CHANGE COLOUR — SOME OF THEM HAVE AN AMAZING GREENY-PURPLE LOOK, AND THE FEMALES DEVELOP A RED STRIPE ON THEIR BACK WHEN THEY'RE READY TO FIND A MATE.

MANTIS SHRIMPS HAVE A BUNCH OF DIFFERENT NICKNAMES THAT RELATE TO THEIR FIERCENESS. IN AUSTRALIA THEY'RE CALLED 'PRAWN KILLERS'. SOMETIMES THEY'RE CALLED 'THUMB SPLITTERS'.

CRITTER ATTRACTIVENESS-OMETER: 8

BECAUSE THEY CAN CHANGE COLOUR, AND BECAUSE OF THEIR EDWARD SCISSORHANDS APPROACH AT VERY FAST SPEEDS. IT'S AMAZEBALLS!

CRITTER ATTRACTIVENESS-OMETER

4

THEY GET EXTRA POINTS FOR BEING THE SECRET AGENTS OF THE BIRD WORLD.

ONE OF THEIR CALLS SOUNDS LIKE A WITCH CACKLING IN THE RUSHES, AND THEY HAVE ANOTHER CALL THAT SOUNDS LIKE A COMB BEING SCRAPED OVER A CREDIT CARD.

THEY CALL MOSTLY AT DUSK AND THROUGH THE NIGHT.

MARSH CRAKE / KOITAREKE

The marsh crake is a really secretive, really elusive, amazing little bird. They're a locally mobile wetland bird found mostly around the damp areas of the South Island. They're seen in other countries around the world, but we have a subspecies here in Aotearoa, called *Porzana pusilla affinis*.

They're very rarely seen, because they live right in the thick of that gorgeous, lush wetland vegetation. This makes them really hard to study (unless you're willing to sit in your gumboots in a wetland in the middle of the night, listening for them!).

They appear stout and dumpy, but that's just because they have a short tail and long legs. They have beautiful plumage, quite spectacular — they look like a Japanese painting, like someone took a brush and dipped it in a few beautiful cinnamons and blacks and silvers and greys and just gently stroked it across the page. Although they do have blood-red eyes, which looks a little freaky!

Marsh crakes nest between September and December. They weave beautiful little grass nests tucked away in the wetland. They lay half a dozen beautiful olive-brown eggs, and they're highly vulnerable to lots of predators.

The main threats to this particular species are habitat loss (New Zealand has lost 90 per cent of its wetlands since European settlement), as well as predators like dogs, mustelids, rats and especially cats. Marsh crakes are also at risk from predators like harrier hawks, but you can learn to live with the predators you've evolved with.

Department of Conservation scientists have been radio-tagging marsh crakes to try to figure out where they go and what they do. They're not migratory like godwits — they don't have a set route that they follow on a seasonal basis — but they are very, very mobile; they follow food, and they follow good habitat — which makes it a challenge to try to manage them!

What's interesting about marsh crakes is that they don't necessarily have to live on conservation land — if private landowners look after their little wetlands on their farms, we can probably provide quite a large area of habitat for them.

MERCURY ISLANDS TUSKED WĒTĀ

Even though they look a bit scary — they've been described as 'the mammoths of the invertebrate world', for pretty obvious reasons — Mercury Islands tusked wētā are quite docile. They're one of the largest insects we've got (our biggest is the wētāpunga of Te Hauturu-o-Toi/Little Barrier Island; the heaviest insect in the world, weighing about the same as a song thrush) and can fill up the palm of an adult's hand. The males have big tusks which they use for fighting — they lock horns with other males and tip them over, sort of like WWE wrestlers.

Tusked wētā dig burrows and live mostly underground. They're carnivorous; eating lots of other little invertebrates that are running around, as well as, according to researchers, cat food and even fish food if it's on offer.

They're known as Middle Island wētā or Mercury Islands wētā or motuwētā (motu meaning island). They were discovered in pretty low numbers in 1970 on Middle Island in the Mercury Islands group off the Coromandel Peninsula. About 15 years later, scientists considered translocating some of the Middle Island wētā to other islands, as they knew this would be important in boosting numbers, but decided this would be too risky. Instead, they decided to take a few back to Auckland and try breeding them in captivity first before translocating their babies.

Fortunately, the wētā bred very well in captivity, and babies were able to be translocated to about six other islands in the Mercury group. That's lucky, because none of the wild (original) population on Middle Island have been seen in the last 15 years, so it's thought that the wild population was probably only a hair's breadth from becoming extinct. Those scientists probably rescued the entire tusked wētā species from extinction — and they did the whole thing from just one male and two females!

Nowadays, tusked wētā live on a handful of islands. They're tricky to see, as they've developed behaviours to avoid predators such as tuatara (for example, they tend to come out on moonless nights, when it's a bit wetter). But they're doing well — even on very recent visits, scientists have been able to find them.

Tusked wētā lay their eggs in autumn and winter, and they hatch in the spring. They are relatively easy to see: they're oval, and about 1 centimetre long.

CRITTER ATTRACTIVENESS-OMETER

8.5

Because there are different ways to judge attractiveness! These things are just cool!

NATIVE MOLE CRICKET

We think there are probably between 50 and 100 species of mole cricket around the world — they're found on every continent except Antarctica. Our native one is called *Triamescaptor aotea*.

Native mole crickets are rarely seen. They live 10 to 15 centimetres under the ground — hence their name — and they're nocturnal, coming out of their burrows at night. Their numbers are declining, probably because they don't do well in cultivated soil (and you can imagine why — if you live just beneath the surface of the soil, and that soil keeps getting dug up and turned over, dug up and turned over, you're not going to thrive). You'll find them in the lower North Island, including in Hawke's Bay, Whanganui, Manawatū, the Wairarapa and D'Urville Island.

Coming from the cricket-grasshopper-wētā family, most types of mole cricket use their wings to make noise to attract mates . . . except ours don't, because they don't have any wings. So we're not quite sure how they talk to each other, particularly under the ground, where they make these quite complex little chambers. It's a bit of a mystery!

So if other crickets meet their potential mates by making noise with their wings, how do our mole crickets do it? Do they write poetry or leave notes? Well, the jury's still out, but there's a theory that they use the vibrations of the soil as they're moving around in it to communicate, because other species in the family do that.

What about their physiology? Any interesting features? The native mole cricket sort of looks like a wētā, or like one of those long, double-length buses that bend in the middle. They're like crickets in reverse, with short, slender back legs and grunty front legs, with three dactyls (that look like moles' paws) on the front legs for digging. They can move really, really quickly through the soil, and can make their way through about 6 metres of soil per night, feeding on roots, grass grubs and porina caterpillars.

What are they like to eat? Nic's not sure — although her husband, of Ngāpuhi, suspects they're probably great. Increasingly, food producers are looking at insects as protein for humans, and in some parts of the world you can buy canned mole crickets!

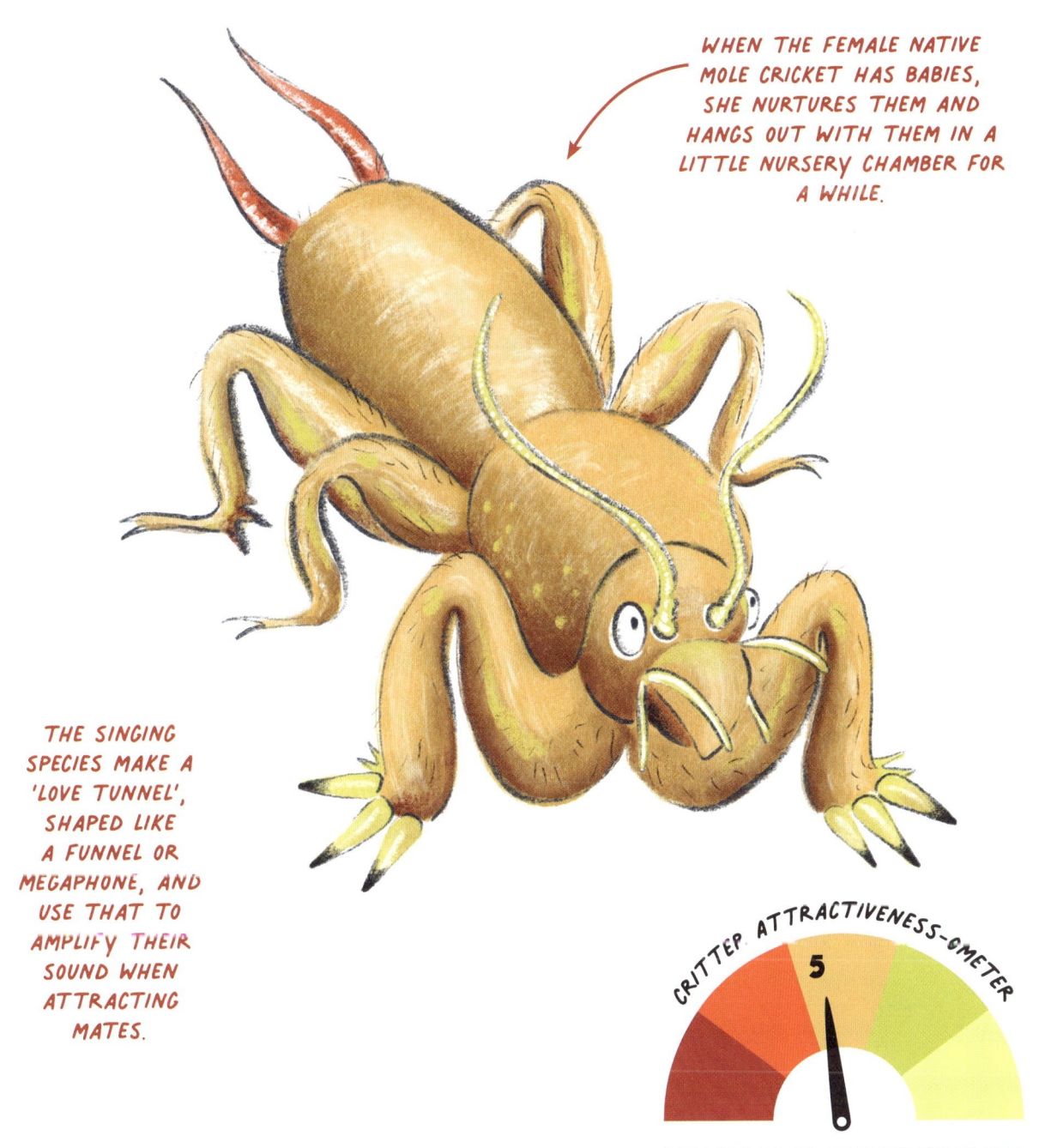

WHEN THE FEMALE NATIVE MOLE CRICKET HAS BABIES, SHE NURTURES THEM AND HANGS OUT WITH THEM IN A LITTLE NURSERY CHAMBER FOR A WHILE.

THE SINGING SPECIES MAKE A 'LOVE TUNNEL', SHAPED LIKE A FUNNEL OR MEGAPHONE, AND USE THAT TO AMPLIFY THEIR SOUND WHEN ATTRACTING MATES.

CRITTER ATTRACTIVENESS-OMETER

5

THEY GET A 5 FOR THEIR EFFORTS TO KEEP OUR SOIL HEALTHY.

CRITTER ATTRACTIVENESS-OMETER: 6

DUE TO THEIR CLEVER CAPTURE EFFORTS.

DESPITE THEIR FEARSOME APPEARANCE, THEY ARE COMPLETELY HARMLESS TO HUMANS.

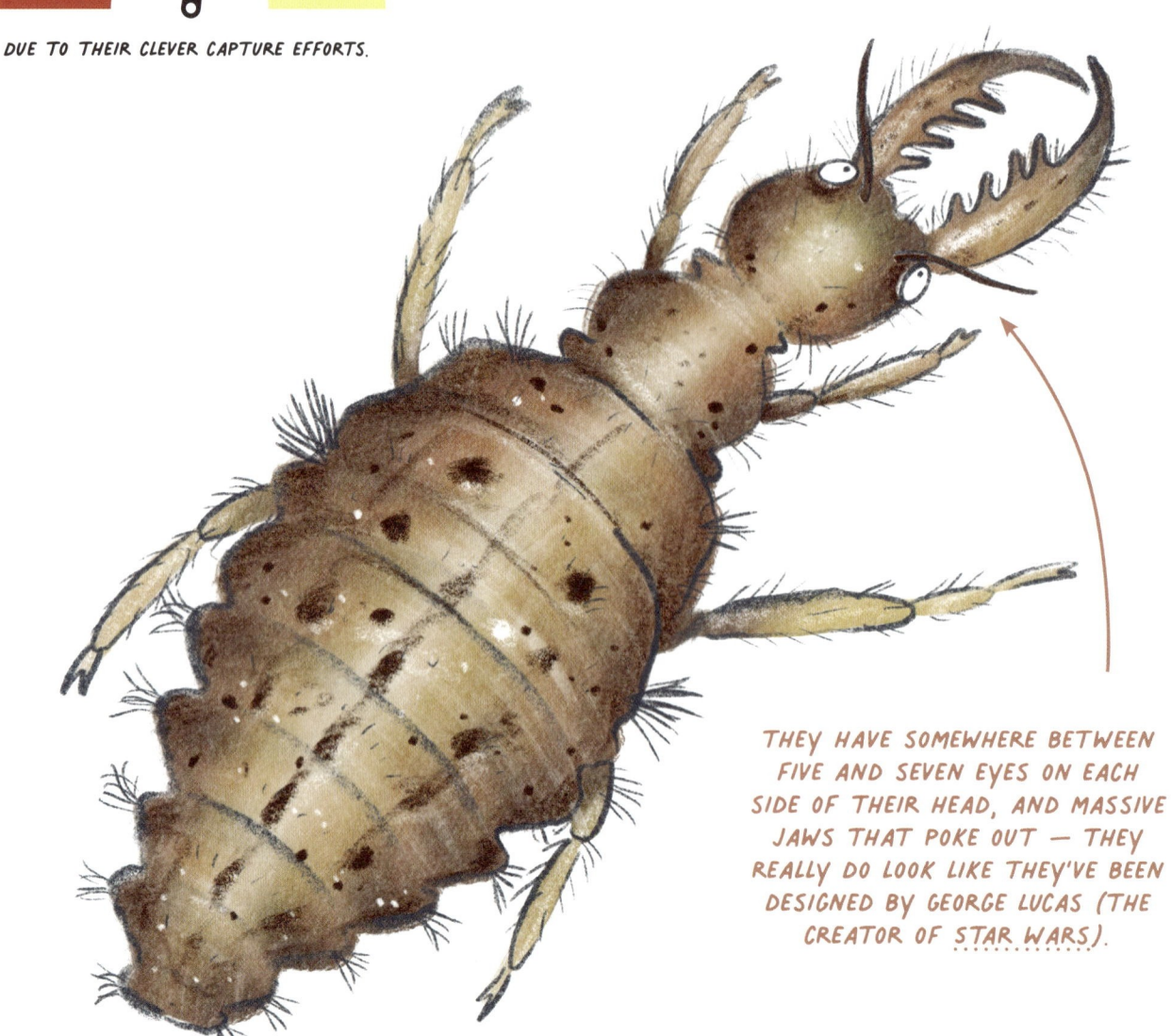

THEY HAVE SOMEWHERE BETWEEN FIVE AND SEVEN EYES ON EACH SIDE OF THEIR HEAD, AND MASSIVE JAWS THAT POKE OUT — THEY REALLY DO LOOK LIKE THEY'VE BEEN DESIGNED BY GEORGE LUCAS (THE CREATOR OF STAR WARS).

NEW ZEALAND ANTLION / KUTU KUTU

If you're a *Star Wars* fan, it's basically the Sarlacc!

In real life, the kutu kutu is New Zealand's only endemic antlion. An antlion is actually the larval stage of a lacewing. (Lacewings kind of look like a damsel fly, those skinny versions of dragonflies — quite a beautiful, fragile-looking insect.) The larva is this short, squat creature with massive jaws.

What they do is they dig a little pit in the sand or in the soil, a couple of centimetres across, and they sit and wait for ants or other insects to fall in at night. Once their victim is in the very clever pit that they've dug, they use their massive jaws to inject venom into it, to paralyse it, then they just hoover it up. They also chuck a bit of sand underneath the ant or insect to help it lose its footing.

They spend a lot of time digging the hole. They crawl backwards, using their abdomen to shovel the soil up. And they also use their head to flick the sand or the soil around — they kind of look like they're doing the East Coast wave!

Another interesting thing is that the antlion just sits underneath its little pit and waits for vibrations; it's not looking for the ant, it just feels something crawl in, and that's when it starts chucking sand up. It's the oldest trick in the book: if you want to trap something, dig a hole! And they've been doing that for a really long time.

There are lots of antlion species worldwide, and about 16 in New Zealand. We think that they're called antlions because they mostly eat ants. In the United States they get called 'doodle bugs', because when they're moving between pits and trying to find a new place to go, they leave these really elaborate little tracks behind them, almost like someone was doodling with a pen. Once someone has pointed one out, they're really easy to spot, which is quite fun.

NEW ZEALAND GLOW WORM

Their scientific name is *Arachnocampa luminosa*, which means something like 'glowing cave spider'. Titiwai is their Māori name, which means 'lights reflected in water'.

Most New Zealanders have probably seen glow worms. You can see them in the Waitomo Caves, as well as in other caves and also along the banks of little creeks and bush tracks all over the country.

Glow worms are neat because they glow that beautiful aqua, blue-green colour. But let's clear something up straight away: they're not a worm! They're actually the larvae of a fungus gnat. We have about 300 species of fungus gnat in Aotearoa, but only the New Zealand glow worm produces light.

They live in tiny little hollow transparent tubes that they make, and they shuffle along inside them (the tubes are horizontal), and hang down threads of 'silk'. Down each thread are these tiny little beads of mucus — a little hanging curtain of silken threads — which they essentially use for fishing! Other little creatures in the cave are attracted to the light, and when they bumble into the threads, the larvae pull them up and eat them! As well as attracting food, their glow also helps them to burn off waste. What you're seeing is bioluminescence — a reaction between the chemicals given off by the glow worm and the oxygen in the air, which creates light. Glow worms can control that light by reducing the oxygen to the light organ (like an eco light!). The ones that live in caves have threads that can hang down up to half a metre (they kind of look like nature's chandelier!). But the ones in the forest tend to be only up to about 5 centimetres long. And that's because outside, if they're too long, they get tangled in the wind and then they're useless.

Once the fungus gnat larvae cocoon themselves into a pupa (a little hanging sac) for

THE ORGAN THAT CREATES THE 'GLOW' IS THE EQUIVALENT OF A HUMAN KIDNEY.

CRITTER ATTRACTIVENESS-OMETER 7.8

BECAUSE THE SUN SHINES OUT OF ITS BUM!

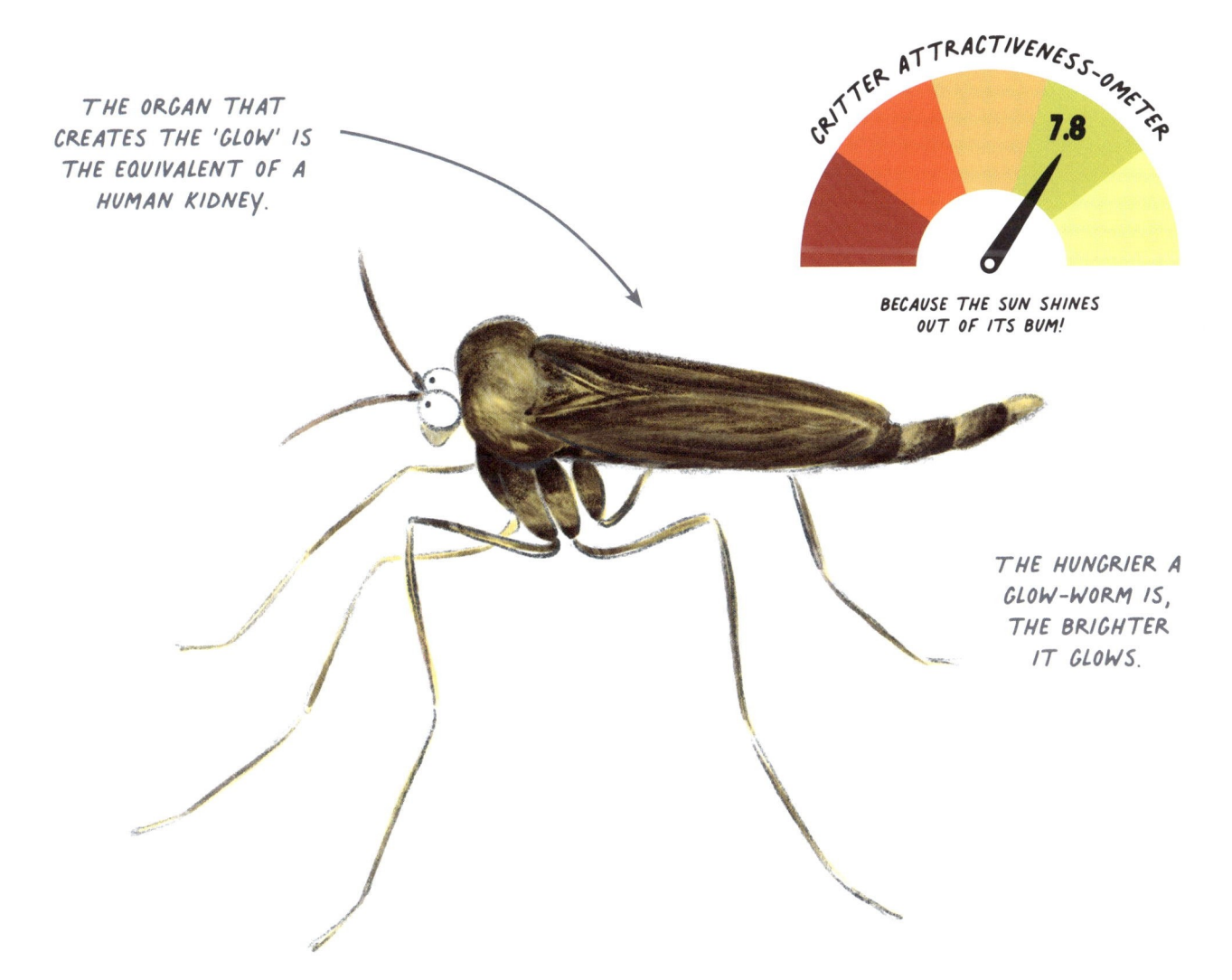

THE HUNGRIER A GLOW-WORM IS, THE BRIGHTER IT GLOWS.

a couple of weeks, they hatch out into a little fly-looking thing (they are part of the fly family) and they only live for three days! They have no mouth, but they do have 'bits', and their whole purpose is to reproduce — so the female will lay eggs, which hatch after about three weeks, and then the cycle starts again.

Glow worms eat little things like midges, mayflies, caddisflies, mosquitos, moths and even little snails or millipedes. When they catch something that's too big, for example when some human or spider blunders into their thread, they can just release it. They very occasionally catch other adult fungus gnats as they're emerging from the pupa, so then there's a little bit of . . . cave cannibalism. They just eat them as well!

NEW ZEALAND LAMPREY

This is a star performer in the 'ugliness' category. We don't really know that much about it, but the New Zealand lamprey, or kanakana/piharau, is pretty amazing.

Lamprey are one of our most primitive species of vertebrates. They don't have bones; they're cartilaginous — kind of like sharks and stingrays. They're a jawless fish species, like the hagfish (see pages 34–35). And they have an incredible mouth with really specialised teeth. Their job is to latch onto a fish or other prey and then just rasp away and suck up the juices and the flesh and the blood. Like something out of a science-fiction movie. Or a vacuum cleaner attachment with teeth!

In their life cycle they move from streams and rivers to the ocean, where they spend many years before heading back to freshwater. We don't really know where they are,

FOR THE FIRST FEW YEARS OF A LAMPREY'S LIFE, THEY ARE BLIND FILTER FEEDERS, WHICH MEANS THEY BURY THEIR HEAD IN THE SEDIMENTS THAT SIT AT THE BOTTOM OF A STREAM AND COLLECT UP ALL THE NUTRIENTS.

TO MĀORI, KANAKANA/PIHARAU ARE A DELICACY AND A TAONGA. THEY CAN BE TRICKY TO CATCH, THOUGH! WHANGANUI IWI CAUGHT KANAKANA/PIHARAU IN A SERIES OF TRAPS CALLED WEIRS. IN SOUTHLAND, PEOPLE SOMETIMES GRABBED THEM BY HAND OFF THE ROCKS AT THE MATAURA FALLS.

CRITTER ATTRACTIVENESS-OMETER

−1

BECAUSE LAMPREY ARE SO OTHERWORLDLY, IT DOESN'T MAKE SENSE FOR THEM TO EVEN ACHIEVE A RATING ON THIS SCALE!

but we think they can probably go very long distances in the ocean (which anyone probably could, if you were hitchhiking by sucking onto another big fish or whale!). Lamprey come back up the rivers to breed in late winter or early spring. We don't really know many places where they spawn, but we think it's probably in forested creeks with stony bottoms, which they need to lay their eggs. There are records from the 1920s, from the Whanganui River, of the larvae being found 240 kilometres upstream!

To Māori, kanakana/piharau are a delicacy and a taonga and they have traditional methods of gathering them. It's difficult, though, because the piharau move at night and the rest of the time they're hiding.

To the untrained eye, the piharau looks a bit like an eel, unless you get quite close to it. They're slimy and have seven gill slots tucked in behind their eyes. They don't even *have* eyes until they're adults. When they're babies, they hatch out somewhere in a creek and then burrow into the substrate and live there for years and just filter-feed.

As the adults head upstream from the sea to breed, they look awesome — they're silver with bright blue racing stripes. They kind of look like those monorail trains that you see overseas! They can be anywhere up to about 60 centimetres long.

What's really cool is that when lamprey come upstream, they climb! They can climb up to 20 metres over waterfalls, using their jaws — almost like a reverse slinky.

About a hundred years ago, they were commonly seen — people might have seen thousands of them slinking up waterfalls, for example. But we don't see that now. We don't know very much about them, but we know that they're probably in trouble due to the state of our waterways, which fill up with sediment because of erosion, so they're probably struggling with their spawning habitat. In the South Island there's been a weird lamprey disease going on, which sadly kills them.

NEW ZEALAND PEA CRAB

These are the little crabs you spot in green-lipped mussels when you open them up — they look like a little pink pea! It's one of our first critters that actually lives inside another critter! It's kind of like the ultimate tiny house!

These crabs are found inside green-lipped mussels and other bivalves, like pipi and oysters and cockles. They're parasites, stealing from the bivalve's table. They take plankton from the gills of the green-lipped mussel, which protects them by providing a really good caravan to live in. The mussels feed by filtering water through their gills, and then the crabs transfer the plankton through to their mouths.

It's interesting because mussels are really hard to open, and so to get out of the mussel, the male crabs tickle them! Then they tickle open other green-lipped mussels so they can get in to mate with the female crabs — they can spend up to 200 minutes tickling a single mussel! The males are flatter and smaller than the females and they have harder shells because they are the ones that leave the mussels, once they've tickled them open, to find a mate.

They're not a threatened species, and lots of people have found pea crabs inside mussels, which is a really nice reminder that all of our wildlife is interconnected. Taking one thing out of an ecosystem often has a ripple effect on another, so we've got to make sure we're aware of those connections and protect all the things, not just one.

It's a risky business being a pea crab. Because apart from the fact that they get eaten by snapper and spotties, the males can also be crushed by the green-lipped mussel's shell while they're trying to get in to mate with the females. And this can be really common. What a way to go!

The male pea crab is not well invested in the relationship, it's fair to say! He comes out when it's dark, finds a mussel with a female inside (probably by smell; by pheromones), tickles the mussel to get in, releases his sperm, then leaves again — and she has to do the rest! Although, when you look at the ratio of female to male mature pea crabs, almost 90 per cent of them are female and only 10 per cent are male (you'd expect this ratio to be 50:50), and scientists believe that most of the males are being crushed on their way through, looking for love.

CRITTER ATTRACTIVENESS-OMETER — 5

BECAUSE THEY'RE BEAUTIFUL AND COOL — THEY KIND OF LOOK LIKE THE BADDIES IN THE OLD SPACE INVADERS ARCADE GAME.

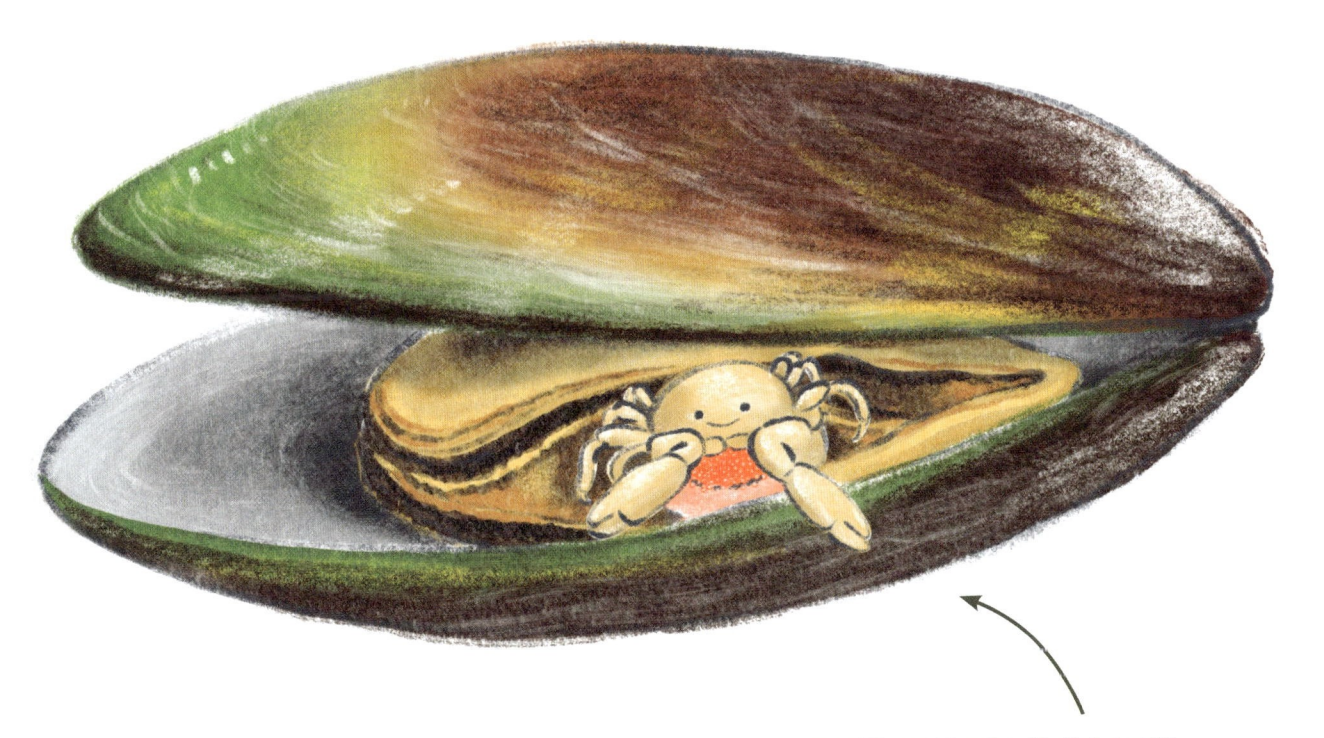

ADULT MALE PEA CRABS MAKE UP AROUND 10 PER CENT OF THE POPULATION, BUT UP TO 90 PER CENT OF ALL ADULT FEMALES CARRY FERTILISED EGGS . . . SO THEY ARE BUSY BOYS!

CRITTER ATTRACTIVENESS-OMETER

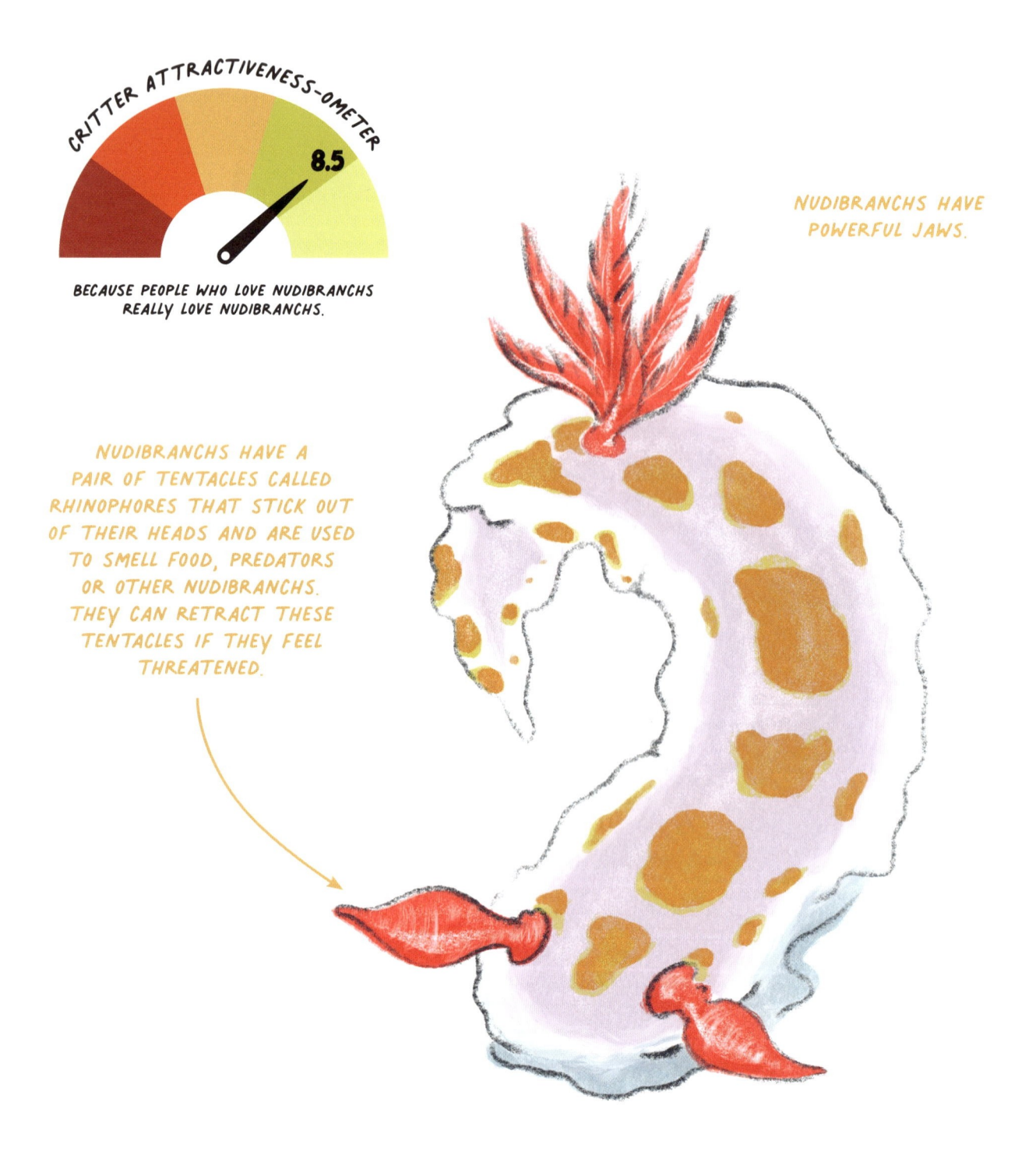

8.5

BECAUSE PEOPLE WHO LOVE NUDIBRANCHS REALLY LOVE NUDIBRANCHS.

NUDIBRANCHS HAVE POWERFUL JAWS.

NUDIBRANCHS HAVE A PAIR OF TENTACLES CALLED RHINOPHORES THAT STICK OUT OF THEIR HEADS AND ARE USED TO SMELL FOOD, PREDATORS OR OTHER NUDIBRANCHS. THEY CAN RETRACT THESE TENTACLES IF THEY FEEL THREATENED.

NUDIBRANCHS

There are many species of nudibranch (pronounced nudi-brank) — about 3000 worldwide, with some even in Antarctica — and we have around 80 species here in Aotearoa. They're not really threatened, but they are quite beautiful.

Nudibranchs are a species of mollusc. Most of us know them as sea slugs, and those of us who are divers or snorkelers may have seen them. They're a type of gastropod, which means 'stomach-footed'. If you think of any of the molluscs, like pāua or limpets, those tend to be gastropods (except not the bivalves or the ones that click together). They're a species of mollusc that has lost its shell. But unlike the grey land slugs that hang around under logs near your house, these marine species are incredible — some of them have ridiculously striking colours. And they lay beautiful-looking, koru-shaped ribbons of eggs.

Nudibranchs are only little (for example, clown nudibranchs are only about 4 centimetres long; others can grow up to about 20 centimetres long). Nudibranch means 'naked gills', and if you look at them, nudibranchs have these feathery appendages on them — these create extra surface area for the nudibranchs to process oxygen to breathe.

It can be hard to describe a nudibranch, because they all look so different, as they come in different sizes, shapes and colours.

They're carnivores, and some of them have horn-looking things on the front of their head. Nudibranchs can't see very well, but they use these horns for olfaction: smelling and detecting chemicals and changes in the water.

What's really cool about a lot of species of nudibranch is that they can eat things that have toxins in them, and they then use those toxins to make themselves not taste very good to predators that might eat them. The Jason's nudibranch, which is a beautiful, pink-and-white, feathery-looking creature, is able to ingest poisonous nematocysts taken from their prey (nematocysts are tiny, tiny capsules produced by some sea animals, such as jellyfish, coral and sea anemones that contain a miniscule barb or harpoon filled with venom).

After being eaten, the nematocysts pass through the nudibranch, and sometimes out into their feathery gills; both the bright colours of the nudibranchs (a near-universal warning sign in animals to predators: 'Don't eat me; I taste bad or am poisonous') and the poison of the nematocysts protects the nudibranchs from being eaten. If an animal was colour-blind and took a bite of a nudibranch, it would probably go, 'Ew, I'm not having that!' As an animal, if you don't have an exoskeleton or shell, then being poisonous can be a good survival method.

PERIPATUS / NGĀOKEOKE / VELVET WORM / WALKING WORM

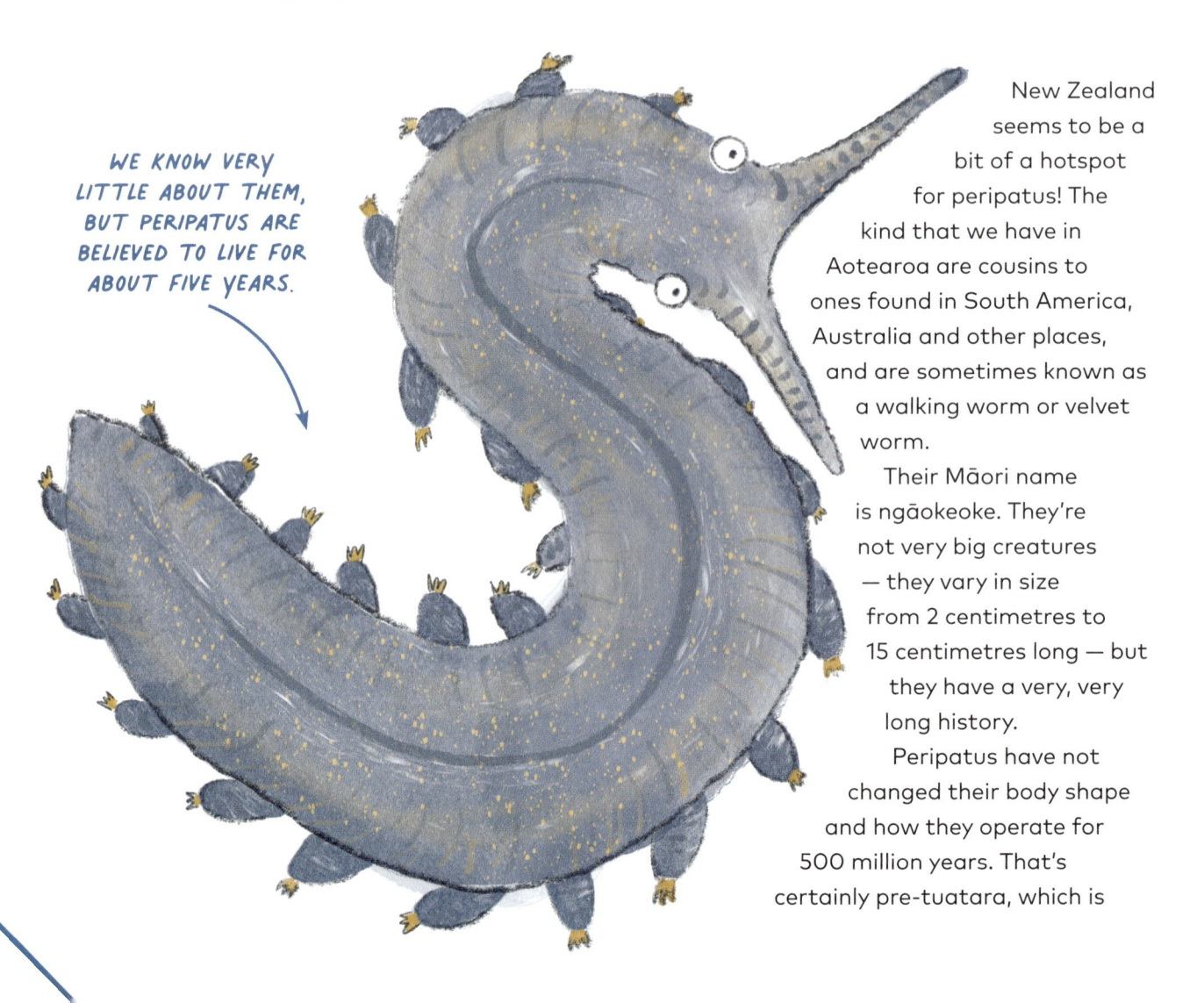

WE KNOW VERY LITTLE ABOUT THEM, BUT PERIPATUS ARE BELIEVED TO LIVE FOR ABOUT FIVE YEARS.

New Zealand seems to be a bit of a hotspot for peripatus! The kind that we have in Aotearoa are cousins to ones found in South America, Australia and other places, and are sometimes known as a walking worm or velvet worm.

Their Māori name is ngāokeoke. They're not very big creatures — they vary in size from 2 centimetres to 15 centimetres long — but they have a very, very long history.

Peripatus have not changed their body shape and how they operate for 500 million years. That's certainly pre-tuatara, which is

SOME SPECIES LAY EGGS, BUT MOST BEAR LIVE YOUNG. THEY CAN PRODUCE UP TO 20 OFFSPRING EACH YEAR.

CRITTER ATTRACTIVENESS-OMETER

8.5

BECAUSE THEY CAN COME IN FLUORO COLOURS LIKE PURPLE AND ORANGE.

often thought of as a living dinosaur. Their ancestors were swimming around in the ocean looking almost exactly like the peripatus we have fossicking around in the bush and, occasionally, the garden today.

Despite its 'walking worm' name, they're not actually worms. They're not an insect either — they're somewhere in the middle, and can't be classified either way. They do look like a caterpillar — they're long, velvety, kind of bumpy-looking creatures with antennae and lots of stumpy, wee, fluid-filled legs with claws on the end.

We might not have lions stalking the savannah, but here in New Zealand we have this incredible predator weaving its way through our forests at night. Peripatus have two turrets, one on each side of their head, and when they see a little creature that they want to eat, like a little beetle, they shoot slime out of these turrets — over quite a distance. As soon as the slime lands on their chosen prey, it instantly hardens, like superglue. Then the peripatus just sneaks up on top of it and eats both the prey and the slime, recycling the slime. It's amazing!

What sorts of insects does it eat? Little beetles, little flies, little spiders; any little invertebrate that it finds in the moist leaf-litter on the forest floor.

We have about nine species here in Aotearoa. Probably the most famous ones are the Dunedin variety, who have their own reserve. In the suburb Caversham, there's a big bush reserve that's always had peripatus in it. When the local highway needed to be widened, Forest & Bird and other peripatus-lovers made quite a lot of noise to ensure that plans were made so the peripatus would be OK. Everyone got their heads together and came up with a solution — basically planting more trees next to the existing bush, as well as educating people about the peripatus. It's become an interesting part of what was just going to become another boring highway realignment. Thank goodness for the Dunedin community, who love their peripatus!

RANGATIRA SPIDER

Rangatira Island — also known as South East Island — is part of the Chatham Islands, and it's one of our most special nature reserves. It's probably best known for being the home of the world's last black robins. Rangatira was farmed until the 1960s but somehow rats and cats never made it onto the island, making it a lifeboat for wildlife. As well as its native birdlife, it's also home to the Rangatira spider, which has the conservation status 'At Risk, Relict', because it's found in only 10 per cent of its former range.

Rangatira spiders can grow to 12 centimetres in diameter, including their legs. They're like a revved-up version of a nursery-web spider — they're the ones that make those big, boxy web-nests at the tops of clumps of toetoe, flax and long grass to protect all the tiny spiderlings inside.

Rangatira spiders come out at night. They have really bright 'eyeshine' — if you flash a torch at one, you can spot its eyes from 20 metres away! That's pretty impressive.

Their favourite food is wētā, but they don't catch them in webs — they pounce on them while out hunting at night — *blammo!* — onto the wētā!

Female Rangatira spiders are bigger than males; their bodies can be up to about 3 centimetres long, while the males are about 2.5 centimetres long. And then they have these huge legs as well! You'd really know about it if one crawled up your leg.

They are doing OK on pest-free Rangatira Island but sadly they have disappeared from nearby Pitt Island, where they were once common, because Pitt Island has mice, which eat the giant spiders. That's a great example of why predator-free islands are important — not only to protect big, fluffy-feathered things but also the big eight-legged things as well.

Some species of spiders disperse by 'ballooning' — remember Charlotte's babies in *Charlotte's Web*? They climbed to the top of a fencepost, poked their bums in the air, let out a trail of silk and drifted off in the wind. That's called ballooning. We think that Rangatira spiders probably balloon too, because in the lab we have seen the spiderlings poking their bottoms up in a fake breeze. We think they probably can make the short balloon trip between Rangatira Island and nearby Pitt and Mangere islands. So if we could manage to clear Pitt Island of predators, we could have a new home for them, and they'd probably just appear there by themselves.

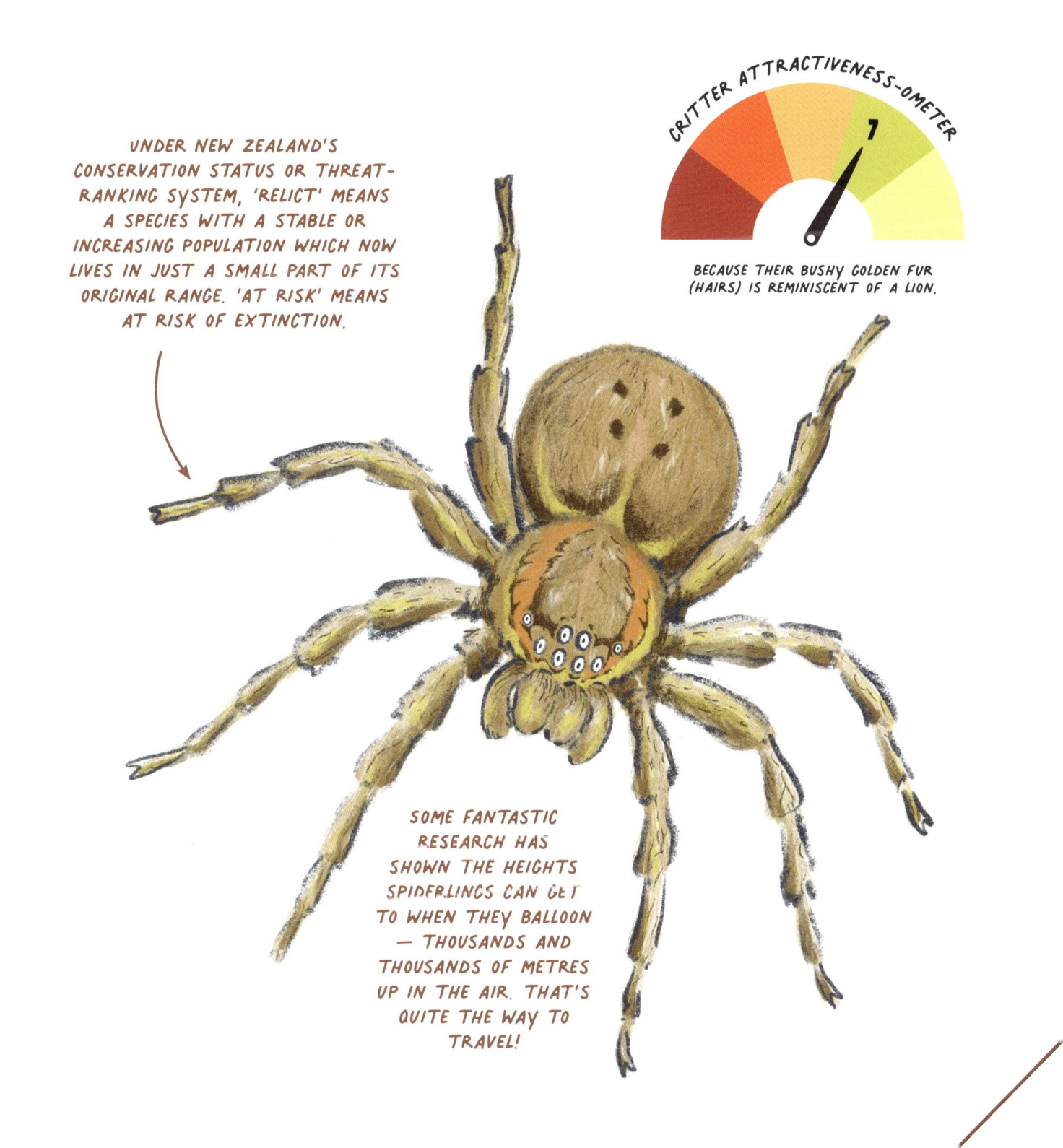

UNDER NEW ZEALAND'S CONSERVATION STATUS OR THREAT-RANKING SYSTEM, 'RELICT' MEANS A SPECIES WITH A STABLE OR INCREASING POPULATION WHICH NOW LIVES IN JUST A SMALL PART OF ITS ORIGINAL RANGE. 'AT RISK' MEANS AT RISK OF EXTINCTION.

CRITTER ATTRACTIVENESS-OMETER

7

BECAUSE THEIR BUSHY GOLDEN FUR (HAIRS) IS REMINISCENT OF A LION.

SOME FANTASTIC RESEARCH HAS SHOWN THE HEIGHTS SPIDERLINGS CAN GET TO WHEN THEY BALLOON — THOUSANDS AND THOUSANDS OF METRES UP IN THE AIR. THAT'S QUITE THE WAY TO TRAVEL!

ALTHOUGH THEY ARE CALLED GRASSHOPPERS, THEY DON'T LIVE ON GRASS, AND THEY DON'T HOP VERY WELL.

CRITTER ATTRACTIVENESS-OMETER

5

NIC LIKES THEM SO MUCH SHE COULD HAPPILY GIVE THEM A SCORE OF 100, BUT SEEING AS WE'RE RATING BY PHYSICAL ATTRACTIVENESS OUT OF 10, SHE GIVES THEM A 5.

A SPECIALLY DESIGNED PREDATOR-PROOF FENCE HAS BEEN INSTALLED IN PART OF THE MACKENZIE BASIN TO KEEP OUT HEDGEHOGS, RODENTS AND MUSTELIDS THAT MIGHT PREY ON THE GRASSHOPPERS.

ROBUST GRASSHOPPER

These grasshoppers are found only in the Mackenzie Basin in the South Island. They're named mostly for their appearance, because they have really big 'shoulders' (if grasshoppers had shoulders), but also because they're tough — they can handle being translocated (moved) to other suitable habitats and survive in a range of temperatures, down to almost −20 degrees Celsius. They're like the Dwayne 'The Rock' Johnson of the insect world!

Robust grasshoppers are specially adapted to their habitat, and are only found in really dry, arid areas, such as river flats and terraces. As a consequence, they're also a threatened species.

They're cool to look at and quite large, as far as insects go — up to 4 centimetres long. The females are much larger than the males (generally about twice the size).

Robust grasshoppers are hard to spot — until one jumps up right in front of your face. They come in a variety of colours, which allows them to camouflage and blend cleverly into their environment.

Like all of our wildlife native to Aotearoa, the robust grasshopper has evolved to deal with avian (bird) predators — ones that hunt by sight. Their camouflage helps the grasshoppers to hide from birds, and they'll also freeze if they think they've been spotted. However, the mammals we've introduced more recently to Aotearoa hunt by smell, so unfortunately the freeze response doesn't help the grasshoppers — it just means predators don't have to walk as far to get them! Predators that feast on robust grasshoppers include animals that we don't necessarily think of in this way, such as hedgehogs.

Like a lot of our threatened species, robust grasshoppers are also missing out on habitat. There's been a lot of habitat change in the Mackenzie Country — a lot of conversion of high-country desert, which they've evolved to exist in, into irrigated pasture farmland — so they are running out of suitable places to live. When you combine that with the impact of predators, the robust grasshopper is in a spot of bother.

SEABIRD TICK

New Zealand is the seabird capital of the world — we have the highest number of breeding species of albatrosses, petrels, shearwaters and penguins on the planet. One of the albatross's passengers is the seabird tick. It's one of 10 species of tick found here in Aotearoa, and lives on a range of albatross species.

A tick is a hemophage, which is a code word for a blood-sucker or vampire. In every stage of its life cycle, except when it's an egg, it has to drink blood to survive.

This particular species has been described as the vampire of the seabirds. They basically just cling onto a bird, usually in a soft spot where they can get their teeth through the skin, and just hang in there until they're completely engorged with blood.

These ticks must really get around! Studies of wandering albatross species have shown that this species can travel 170,000 kilometres in their lifetime — that's nearly halfway to the moon — and all on a 3-metre wingspan! Imagine the things you'd see if you were a tick on that journey!

Life for an albatross isn't that easy, however, which means that life for the tick can also be challenging. The albatross has the double-edged sword of breeding on land and feeding at sea. On land they have challenges, such as climate change (our weather is getting hotter over summer, and albatross eggs and chicks can 'cook' in the heat), as well as predators.

Out at sea they are up against huge storms and wild weather (also caused by climate change), as well as the fishing industry. Albatrosses are opportunists, following fishing boats in the hope of catching a meal, and boats using longlines can accidentally catch the birds. It's pretty terrible — they essentially get dragged under the water and drown. If an adult breeding bird is taken out by a longline, the overall impact on that population is *really* significant — it's the breeding birds that are the most valuable to the survival of the species.

The 'vampire of the seabirds' tick, *Ixodes auritulus zealandicus*, is a 'hard' tick — it has a hard, shiny shell. They have four life stages, hatching from an egg into a six-legged larva, then they have their first blood meal, grow two more legs and become a nymph, then they eventually become an adult.

They're not likely to impact us but it is worth noting — because we get all grossed out about parasites — that half of all species of living things in the world are parasites!

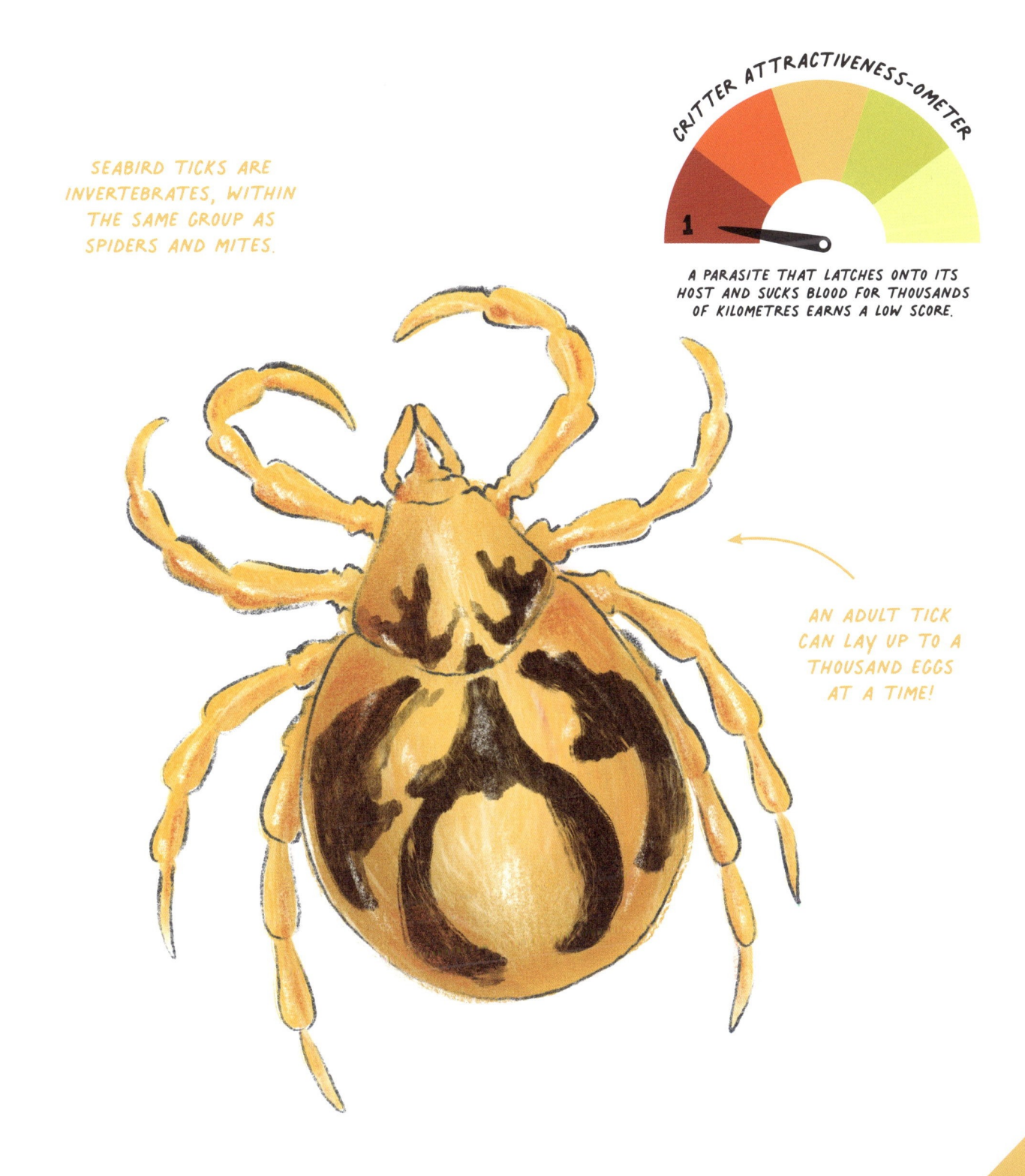

SEABIRD TICKS ARE INVERTEBRATES, WITHIN THE SAME GROUP AS SPIDERS AND MITES.

CRITTER ATTRACTIVENESS-OMETER

1

A PARASITE THAT LATCHES ONTO ITS HOST AND SUCKS BLOOD FOR THOUSANDS OF KILOMETRES EARNS A LOW SCORE.

AN ADULT TICK CAN LAY UP TO A THOUSAND EGGS AT A TIME!

CRITTER ATTRACTIVENESS-OMETER

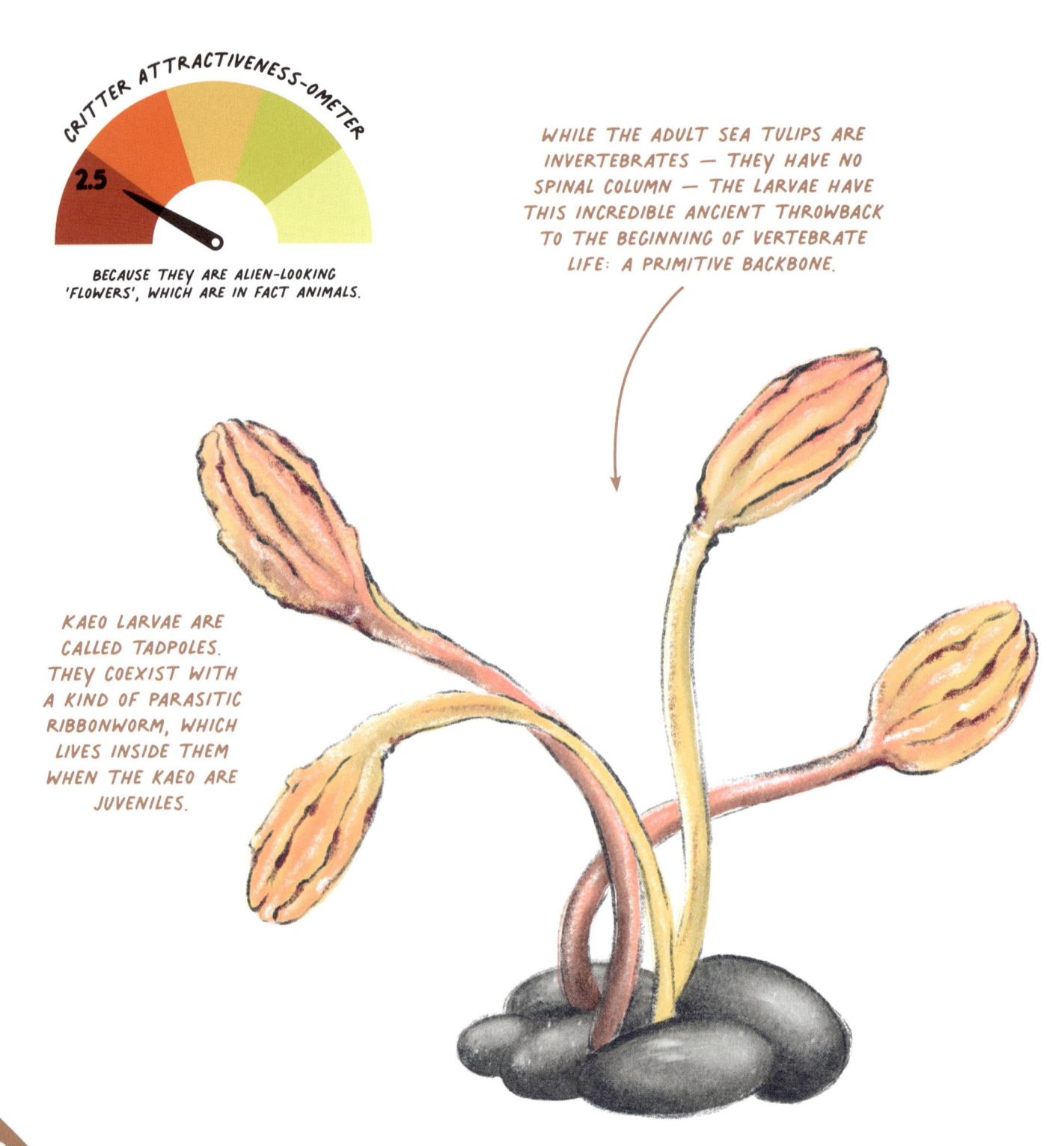

2.5

BECAUSE THEY ARE ALIEN-LOOKING 'FLOWERS', WHICH ARE IN FACT ANIMALS.

WHILE THE ADULT SEA TULIPS ARE INVERTEBRATES — THEY HAVE NO SPINAL COLUMN — THE LARVAE HAVE THIS INCREDIBLE ANCIENT THROWBACK TO THE BEGINNING OF VERTEBRATE LIFE: A PRIMITIVE BACKBONE.

KAEO LARVAE ARE CALLED TADPOLES. THEY COEXIST WITH A KIND OF PARASITIC RIBBONWORM, WHICH LIVES INSIDE THEM WHEN THE KAEO ARE JUVENILES.

SEA SQUIRT OR SEA TULIP / KAEO

One of their common names is sea tulip, and that's because it's almost like someone threw a bunch of slightly wrinkly-looking damp tulips down on the sand. But they're not a flower — they are a filter-feeding invertebrate.

They have this big, long stalk, like a flower, and they attach themselves to rocks in underwater kelp forests. They suck in the salt water and capture any bits of plankton that they can, with what turns out to be quite a complex gut system for an animal that looks exactly like a plant!

Where would you find a sea tulip? They can grow at depths of greater than 30 metres, but are mostly found in the high-energy, dynamic environment where the tide crashes in and out — anywhere they can attach themselves to rocks and there's a big coastal surge, but they do live in quieter harbour waters as well. You'll often see them washed up on beaches after big storms, after they've been ripped off and hurled up on the beach. (When Nic sees them on the beach, she tries to help them by throwing them back into the sea.)

They're pretty cool-looking creatures — they have an almost human-heart-shaped head (which is also their stomach) attached to their long stalk. It's all purple and wrinkly, like something that's fallen out of a UFO. Very alien-like! Inside this funny-looking, giant-raisin-shaped head/stomach, they have quite a complex stomach arrangement called a 'pharangeal basket', in which they catch plankton.

They only live for about one year, before they breed, produce baby squirts and die, and the circle of life starts again.

Fish, sea urchins and starfish all eat sea squirts under the water. Another threat is an invasive species of sea squirt, which can take over their habitat. So it's a short and potentially challenging life for this animal that looks like a plant.

SINBAD SKINK

Despite its name, the Sinbad skink isn't something out of the *Arabian Nights* — it's found in the Sinbad Gully in Fiordland. The gully is an accidental sanctuary, which has been preserved because of its enormous, steep, rocky walls on three sides and ocean on the fourth. It has become a sort of Lost World for native wildlife.

We think the gully was named by a young sailor travelling through Milford Sound/Piopiotahi in 1877, called Donald Sutherland. He was probably looking through the entrance to the valley and thinking of the tale of Sinbad the Sailor and the Valley of the Diamonds. What's beautiful about that is that the treasures or taonga of the Sinbad Gully turned out not to be diamonds, but instead its amazing wildlife.

Over time scientists, rangers and other experts have found weird-looking wētā, rock wrens, kea, whio and the last kākāpō to ever be found on the mainland in Aotearoa. It's a very special place.

And this is a very special skink. The Sinbad skink was only discovered in 2004, and it was found, much to the surprise of the researchers involved, hanging on a rockface way up high. This is how it got its Māori name pikitanga, which means mountain climber.

It's one of only two alpine skinks in Fiordland. To give you an idea of its high-rise lifestyle, it's found 1200 metres above sea level.

It's very beautiful, with wonderful glossy colouring that moves from green through to gold through to maroon, and its belly is bright orange. And even though they live at the top of the basically vertical habitat of the Sinbad Gully, we think that they probably give birth to live young, because all of the other species in this genus do as well — which is quite unusual for skinks elsewhere in the world, which tend to lay eggs.

There is another species of lizard up there (the cascade gecko), existing at altitudes so high that scientists actually find them with the ends of their toes frozen! We humans think we're so hardy, but there are creatures out there existing every day in habitats and climates that we couldn't possibly dream of surviving in for more than 24 hours.

Thankfully there's some amazing conservation work going on in Sinbad Gully, including a big project trapping stoats, to help save its amazing wildlife. And that's protecting those last remaining jewels of the Valley of the Diamonds.

As well as being at high altitude, the Sinbad Valley receives 12 metres of rainfall a year! It's very other-worldly — and very wet!

CRITTER ATTRACTIVENESS-OMETER

8

For being a living jewel that shines even in the toughest of terrains.

CRITTER ATTRACTIVENESS-OMETER

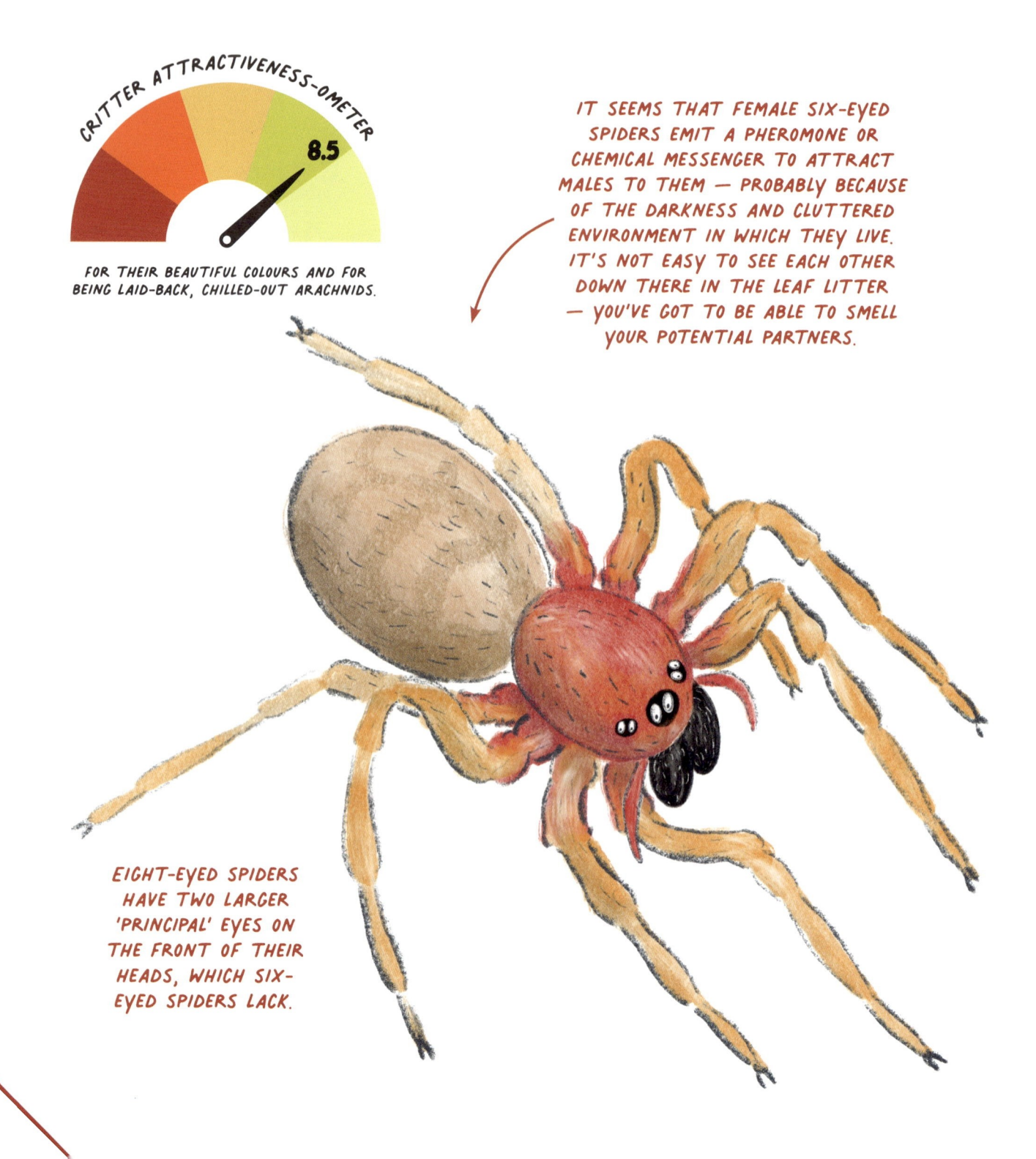

8.5

FOR THEIR BEAUTIFUL COLOURS AND FOR BEING LAID-BACK, CHILLED-OUT ARACHNIDS.

IT SEEMS THAT FEMALE SIX-EYED SPIDERS EMIT A PHEROMONE OR CHEMICAL MESSENGER TO ATTRACT MALES TO THEM — PROBABLY BECAUSE OF THE DARKNESS AND CLUTTERED ENVIRONMENT IN WHICH THEY LIVE. IT'S NOT EASY TO SEE EACH OTHER DOWN THERE IN THE LEAF LITTER — YOU'VE GOT TO BE ABLE TO SMELL YOUR POTENTIAL PARTNERS.

EIGHT-EYED SPIDERS HAVE TWO LARGER 'PRINCIPAL' EYES ON THE FRONT OF THEIR HEADS, WHICH SIX-EYED SPIDERS LACK.

SIX-EYED SPIDER

Most spiders have eight eyes as well as eight legs — but not this one. It's one of a group of six-eyed spiders.

The endemic spider *Periegops suterii* is found exclusively on Banks Peninsula near Christchurch. It used to be found in other places too, including Riccarton Bush, but it has not been seen there for several years. They're not a scary spider at all — they're quite slow-moving and don't jump or scurry.

Having eight eyes is a feature derived through evolution: it's the basic, bog-standard format for spiders. Spider eyes have only one lens (unlike insects, which have compound eyes — a whole mass of lenses all compacted together). The eyes are in groups, so the spider can see out the front of its body, and out the sides.

The eyes of these spiders are extremely good at collecting light in dark environments. This is handy, because they live in the leaf litter and beneath logs in forested areas. They don't need three-dimensional depth of-field vision like humans have, for example; they really just need to be able to see their prey.

They're quite distinctive from other spiders. The six-eyed spider is a honey-yellowish colour, with a darker abdomen with three stripes and a darker band down the centre. This abdomen is similar in shape to a whitetail spider's. They have fairly large chelicerae, which are the mouthparts that hold their fangs. And around their head are the six eyes, positioned in pairs and well separated — two on the left, two at the front and two on the right.

We don't know too much about our native spider, but we know that there's a group of spiders in Queensland, Australia, of the same genus, called *Periegops australia*. And we know there's a third population of six-eyed spider, which were thought to be another species, living on the Aldermen Islands off the Coromandel Peninsula, in the North Island. In fact, they are probably the same species, with the two populations being separated by the rise in sea level after the Late Pleistocene. So that's it: there are two or three species within this genus in total, in three quite different places. And piecing together the evolutionary and biogeographic pieces of the puzzle is quite a head-scratcher!

SMEAGOL THE GRAVEL MAGGOT

The delightfully named Smeagol the gravel maggot is one of our nationally critical species. It's essentially a type of sea slug that lives in the interstitial spaces — the gaps in the gravel — on south coast beaches near Wellington. It was discovered in 1979, and was named after the pale, cave-dwelling creature also known as Gollum from J.R.R. Tolkien's *The Lord of the Rings*.

Despite its revolting-sounding name, this gravel maggot is a fascinating little thing. It's a tiny air-breathing slug, related to the slugs and snails of the garden, but it's found in the intertidal zone. It's about 1 centimetre long and is pretty much white, except you can kind of see through into the guts of it.

One species has been found only on Wellington's south coast, but there are four other species in the Smeagol genus — three that live in Australia and one on the Kaikōura coast. With all the uplift caused by the 2016 Kaikōura earthquakes, when the sea floor rose up by 1 metre, we're not quite sure what's happened to the Smeagol gravel maggot there.

In more positive news, in 2022 marine scientists were surprised and delighted to discover a new population of Smeagol in the Hautai Marine Reserve, New Zealand's most remote marine reserve, 85 kilometres south of Haast on the west coast of the South Island.

What does it like to eat? We think it probably feeds on decaying seaweed. It doesn't have a bottom jaw, but it does have tiny little teeth (which in the snail world are called radula), which it uses to scrape food off the surface of stones, too.

Really, we don't know much about it except that it's got a wonderful name. And because it is so restricted in terms of habitat, that immediately bumps it right up our threatened species list.

Why doesn't it just find some other beaches to hang out on? Well, part of the issue, like for many of our other snails and slugs around New Zealand, is that it doesn't move very far or very fast, plus its ability to spread far and wide is limited by the fact that it's only 1 centimetre long!

SMEAGOL THE GRAVEL MAGGOT WAS THE REASON THAT 'CRITTER OF THE WEEK' STARTED ON RADIO NZ IN 2015. NIC TOLD JESSE IN AN INTERVIEW THAT NO ONE CARED ABOUT CREATURES SUCH AS SMEAGOL, AND CRITTER WAS BORN!

CRITTER ATTRACTIVENESS-OMETER

1

SMEAGOL WAS THE CATALYST FOR 'CRITTER OF THE WEEK' AND THEREFORE DESERVES THE BEST (WORST) CRITTER SCORE.

SCIENTISTS THINK THAT SMEAGOL DOESN'T DISPERSE LARVAE INTO THE SEA LIKE OTHER SEA SLUGS DO, WHICH MIGHT BE A KEY REASON SMEAGOL HASN'T SPREAD FAR AND WIDE.

STRIPED SKINK

ALL NATIVE LIZARDS ARE FULLY PROTECTED UNDER THE WILDLIFE ACT 1953, WHICH MEANS IT'S ILLEGAL TO CATCH OR KILL THEM.

The defining feature of our native skinks is that, unlike these little lizards everywhere else in the world, nearly every species in Aotearoa is viviparous — they give birth to live young (except for one that lives on northern offshore islands, called Suter's skink). Other skink species, particularly in warm areas, find the best strategy is to lay some eggs, run off, find another mate, lay some more eggs, etc. In Aotearoa, where our climate is just that little bit more temperate, the best strategy is to keep your developing babies inside you, where the temperature is slightly warmer than what's

STRIPED SKINKS HAVE BEEN FOUND IN TREES AS HIGH AS 22 METRES TALL. COMPARED TO OTHER SIMILAR, CLOSELY RELATED SKINKS, THIS SPECIES HAS BEEN SHOWN TO HAVE A MUCH STRONGER INCLINATION TO CLIMB, AND IT WILL CLIMB HIGHER THAN OTHER SKINKS.

CRITTER ATTRACTIVENESS-OMETER: 7

LOVELY LIZARDS WHO ENJOY A HIGH-RISE LIFESTYLE.

around you. Our native geckos do this too, but while geckos have twins, striped skinks can have up to eight babies, which is a whole different ball-game! It also bodes well for their continued survival.

The striped skink is little, only about 7.5 centimetres long, with a big, beautiful stripe down each side. It primarily lives in the treetops, or canopies, of our forests. Scientists think they're probably up there 100 per cent of the time, which presents all kinds of problems around where to find them and how to look after them.

While striped skinks have been found right throughout the central North Island, up to Aotea/Great Barrier and Te Hauturu-o-Toi/Little Barrier islands in the Hauraki Gulf, they're one of our least-known and rarely seen lizards — there are only about 150 recorded sightings of them. So we have no idea how many there are or even where they are. But we know they need to live high in the trees, and we've trashed quite a lot of our native forest over the past 200 or so years, so habitat loss has probably been a major factor in their decline.

Living up high like that could be some sort of defence against ground-dwelling predators — unless you meet a ship rat. Unlike other types of rats, ship rats can get to the tops of the tallest trees and to the ends of the thinnest branches.

We know that striped skinks also need really moist habitats, as they're really susceptible to dehydration. Places like Waipoua Forest in Northland, with those enormous kiekie (which are epiphytes — hitchhiker plants that grow in the tops of trees) growing high up the kauri, probably offer these little skinks a great place to live. Sadly, most of the times we've found them is when big trees are cut or fall down, and the skinks are seen to skitter away when the top of the tree hits the ground. Which begs the question: what *else* is going on up there? It's kind of like space — we know very little about life in the canopy of the ancient New Zealand forest.

CRITTER ATTRACTIVENESS-OMETER

4

FOR SHEER WEIRDNESS POINTS, THEY'D BE OFF THE SCALE. BUT FOR ATTRACTIVENESS? 4.

NO MALE TADPOLE SHRIMPS HAVE EVER BEEN FOUND. IT SEEMS THAT THEY ARE ALL FEMALE HERMAPHRODITES, WHICH PRODUCE EGGS (CALLED CYSTS) BY THEMSELVES. THESE EGGS CAN BE HIBERNATING IN THE SOIL FOR DECADES, ESPECIALLY DURING DROUGHTS. ONE TADPOLE SHRIMP EGG OVERSEAS HATCHED AFTER BEING KEPT DRY FOR 28 YEARS.

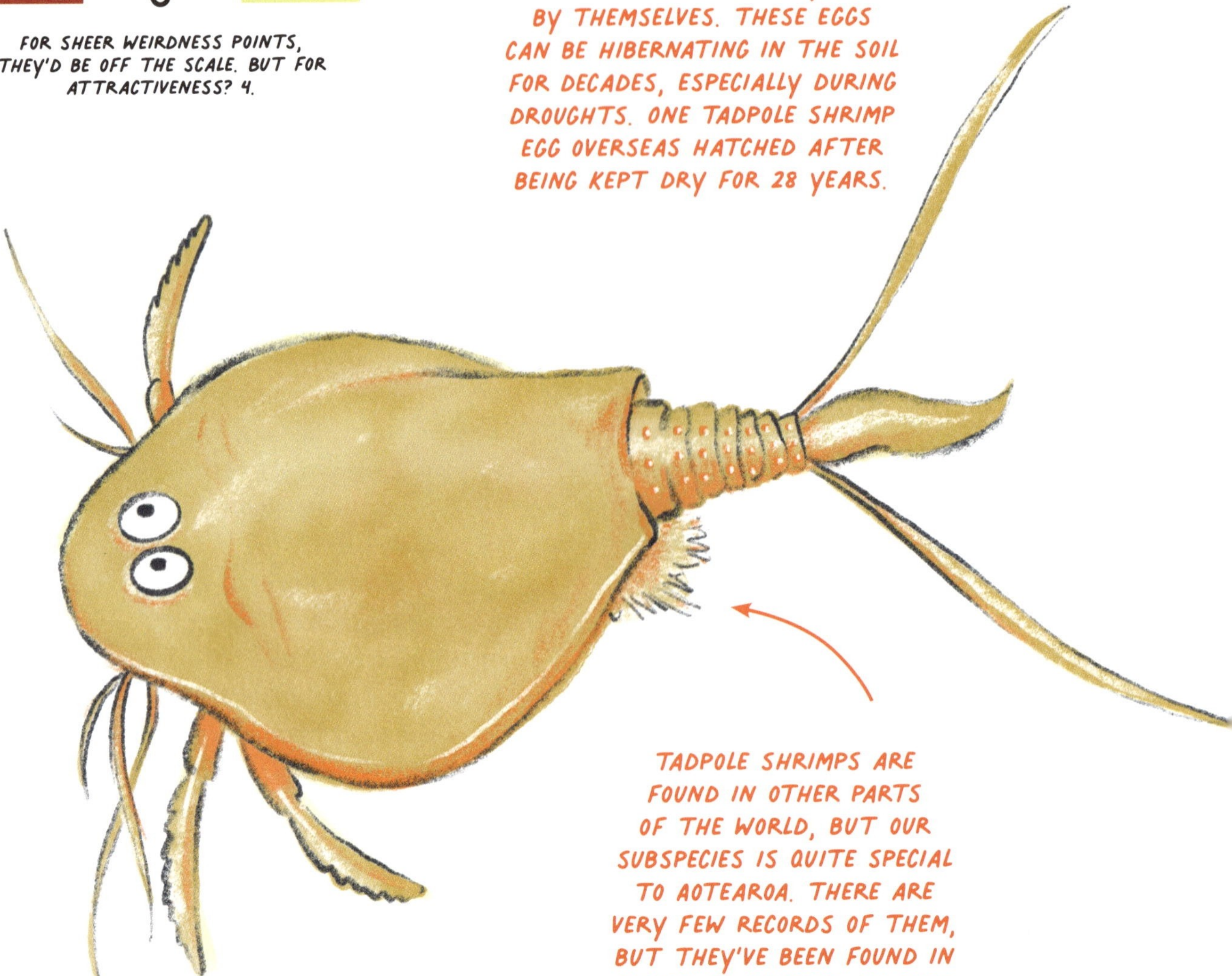

TADPOLE SHRIMPS ARE FOUND IN OTHER PARTS OF THE WORLD, BUT OUR SUBSPECIES IS QUITE SPECIAL TO AOTEAROA. THERE ARE VERY FEW RECORDS OF THEM, BUT THEY'VE BEEN FOUND IN PLACES SCATTERED ALL OVER THE COUNTRY.

TADPOLE SHRIMP / SHIELD SHRIMP

Tadpole shrimps look really cool — kind of like that creepy bug thing that gets inserted into Neo in *The Matrix*. Or like a tiny version of a horseshoe crab. They seem to live in slightly manky, stagnant areas of water (one has been found in the water of an imprint of a horse's hoof), so they're not a species we consider to be an indicator of healthy fresh water, but they periodically disappear and reappear, and we don't know why or where they go.

Tadpole shrimps are 4–6 centimetres long, with a carapace — a shell that sits over the top of their body — and long antennae which fold back behind them. If you look at them from above, they kind of look like tadpoles, but they don't curl around, like shrimps. And despite their name, they're neither a tadpole nor a shrimp.

There's not really anything else like them in the world. And even though they look like horseshoe crabs, they're not related to them at all.

For a while scientists thought that maybe they hadn't really changed for 300 million years. But according to newer molecular studies, the tadpole shrimp *has* changed and re-evolved, and changed and re-evolved, but kept the same shape. Even after many cycles of evolution, it keeps finding that its current form is the right thing to be!

So where are you likely to run into them? They've been found in Canterbury, Otago, Hawke's Bay and the Wairarapa. They're classified as nationally endangered and are threatened with extinction, but we're not sure how much they are at risk because we don't often come across them. And they're not well understood. For example, when they're living in manky puddles, and those puddles disappear, the tadpole shrimps disappear too. Where do they go? Who knows!?

TARDIGRADES

Tardigrades, also known as water bears, have been around for 500 million years or more. They're very, very small (they range from 0.1 of a millimetre to 1 millimetre long). You generally can't see them with the naked eye, but they're really fun to look at under the microscope, especially a fancy electron-scanning one. They've got a sort of sausage-shaped body, four pairs of legs, and a kind of . . . lovable . . . face, like a piglet, with a little snout.

We've known about them for a really long time — they were first discovered by a German scientist in 1773. They are aquatic creatures that generally live on moss and hang out in any wet environment. However, they can live *anywhere*, including . . . in a vacuum, in space.

Given the fact that they can exist in space . . . why would they need to do that unless they'd travelled *through* space on a meteor and landed on Earth that way? While that's a very cool theory, Nic suspects the reason that they could live in space is simply because of their incredible physiological characteristics, which include being able to exist at −272 degrees Celsius, which is pretty close to absolute zero, the coldest conceivable temperature.

What has enabled them to survive anywhere and everywhere — because they're found from the Himalayas down to deep-sea trenches — is that when conditions are not ideal, they suck in their heads and their legs, lie down and become a desiccated creature called a tun. They can exist in that dehydrated state for 30 years! And then you just throw them in water and away they go! (Sort of like those 'Sea Monkeys' some of us used to get as kids . . .)

There are around a thousand species, about 90 of which live in Aotearoa. One of their superpowers — which we recently learned about, thanks to researchers who studied one of the species that's known to be the most hardy (a hardy tardi!) — is that when they do that suspended-animation thing and turn into tuns, essentially they produce a kind of glass which protects all the molecules inside them, until they get wet again.

And then a Japanese research team sequenced the genome of the tardigrade and found out that they have a protein on their DNA that is almost like a forcefield against x-ray radiation. When they then combined that in the lab with some cultured human cells, *the human cells became resistant to x-rays*. How cool is that?

We humans think we're so advanced, that we've reached peak evolution, and yet we don't even come close to what tardigrades can do! Go online and look at videos of them swimming — they're incredible.

Among their common names are 'water bear', as they swim like a bear might walk through the woods, and 'moss piglet'.

The tardigrade 'capital' of New Zealand seems to be Arthur's Pass National Park, where two creeks have yielded more species of tardigrades than any other place in New Zealand.

CRITTER ATTRACTIVENESS-OMETER: 7

Nic thinks they look awesome, like a character from a manga cartoon.

TEA-TREE FINGERS IS QUITE FUSSY: IT GROWS ON THE DEAD BRANCHES OF ITS PREFERRED TREES, BUT ONLY ONES THAT HAVE A 5-CENTIMETRE DIAMETER, AND THEY HAVE TO BE STANDING, AND NOT ON THE GROUND. PICKY, MUCH?!

MYCOLOGISTS (SCIENTISTS WHO STUDY FUNGI) THINK TEA-TREE FINGERS MIGHT BE A PARASITE THAT EATS ANOTHER KIND OF FUNGUS, THE BROWN PAINT FUNGUS. (WHOEVER NAMED THAT ONE WASN'T FEELING PARTICULARLY INSPIRED THAT DAY!)

CRITTER ATTRACTIVENESS-OMETER

2

EVEN AS FUNGI GO, THIS ONE IS PRETTY GROSS AND ALSO HAS A MATCHING NAME.

TEA-TREE FINGERS

Tea-tree fingers (*Hypocreopsis amplectens*) is an endangered fungus. It clasps the dead branches of mānuka like a zombie hand. It kind of looks like someone threw a brown splodge really hard at a branch and it just went *splat!* And it's really, really rare — that's quite important to note.

Fungi are the second largest kingdom of living things on the planet. But we've hardly named any of them, we've hardly identified any of them, and, more importantly, we often don't categorise them or protect them. But this one is nationally critical, so you can pop it into the same category as kākāpō.

It's only known from about half a dozen sites in New Zealand and Australia. Australia's got the jump on us in terms of trying to look after it and protect it, though. Australia has a 'fungi map', where members of the public can report sightings of fungi, which gets a lot of use. Maybe we need one too? You can use the iNaturalist site in the meantime.

It's described as 'crust-like', because it creates this sort of crunchy layer of gangly 'fingers' that go over the mānuka branch. They may look, to the casual observer, like part of a dead old tree, but it's a thriving organism that's living its best life in its favoured habitat.

It was first discovered in Canterbury, in Arthur's Pass, back in 1983. It was found in Australia about nine years later, but it wasn't scientifically described until 2007, so it's pretty new to the science world. It's also been found in the Hanmer Forest Park. But if you see it, please don't collect it! Take a picture and put it on iNaturalist for now, until we get a fungi map. That way we can get a better picture of where they are.

As we know, all living things are connected, including humans, and we just don't know enough about this particular fungus and what its role is. As we learn more about fungi, we find that they have, for example, amazing medicinal properties, or that without them, a particular species of tree can't breed, which means that the birds that rely on that tree might not survive. So tea-tree fingers might be little, with its zombie digits, but it's equally important as many other larger and more beautiful things.

TEVIOT FLATHEAD GALAXIAS

THEY HAVE VERY STRONG FINS, SO IF YOU PUT A YOUNG TEVIOT GALAXIAS IN YOUR HAND, IT CAN CRAWL ACROSS IT LIKE A LIZARD!

These are one of our beautiful native freshwater fish. They're considered nationally critical, which puts them in the same category as Māui dolphins. They're found only in a 2-hectare area near the Teviot River in Central Otago in the South Island. Most of the sites they are found in are streams and wetland on private land, so the key to the survival of this particular fish is the passion and the good nature of the farmers in the area who have them on their property. Fortunately, there are some fantastic landowners who are really excited about the fact that they've got these wee fish on their farms, and don't want to let them go extinct.

THE GALAXIID FAMILY WAS GIVEN THEIR NAME BECAUSE THEY HAVE A BEAUTIFUL SMATTERING OF GOLDEN FLECKS ON THEIR BACK THAT EARLY SCIENTISTS THOUGHT LOOKED LIKE A GALAXY OF STARS (WHICH IS A BIT MORE IMAGINATIVE AND POETIC THAN THE NAMING OF MOST SPECIES, PARTICULARLY FISH!).

CRITTER ATTRACTIVENESS-OMETER

4

HARDY WEE FISH WHO RELY ON FARMERS FOR THEIR ONGOING SURVIVAL.

The Teviot galaxias belongs to a group of fish called galaxiids. We have both migratory and non-migratory galaxiids in New Zealand — you might be more familiar with the migratory ones, because you've probably eaten their babies in whitebait patties. (As an aside, three out of four 'whitebait' species are on the threatened list as well.) The Teviot galaxias is a non-migratory galaxiid, which means it doesn't head out to sea and back again during its life cycle.

They have a tubular body shape, and although they grow to about 16 centimetres long, they can be really hard to spot (despite being spotty!). They eat little small-stream invertebrates like mayfly and stonefly larvae. The best thing we can do to look after what the galaxiids need to eat is to protect our streams. If you have nice riparian planting, fences to keep out stock, plenty of shade to keep the water temperature cool and little pebbles in your stream (so, not so much sedimentation), then you'll have those little underwater insects that the Teviot galaxias like to eat. Happy habitat, happy insects, happy fish (happy water quality . . . happy farming!).

Another massive threat to these wee guys is that they're eaten by introduced trout. We don't often think of trout as a predator or a conservation problem, but for galaxiids they are a serious threat. Teviot galaxias don't exist anywhere where there are trout — they are only found above natural stream barriers such as waterfalls, which trout can't get up. They've been able to hang on for dear life above the areas that the trout can reach.

Currently there is a plan to create another source of renewable energy by flooding the area where Teviot galaxias are found (the NZ Battery Project), which would mean the loss of their habitat, as well as enabling trout to get to them, which would be game over for the species if that happened. Is it worth it to lose an entire species forever?

CRITTER ATTRACTIVENESS-OMETER

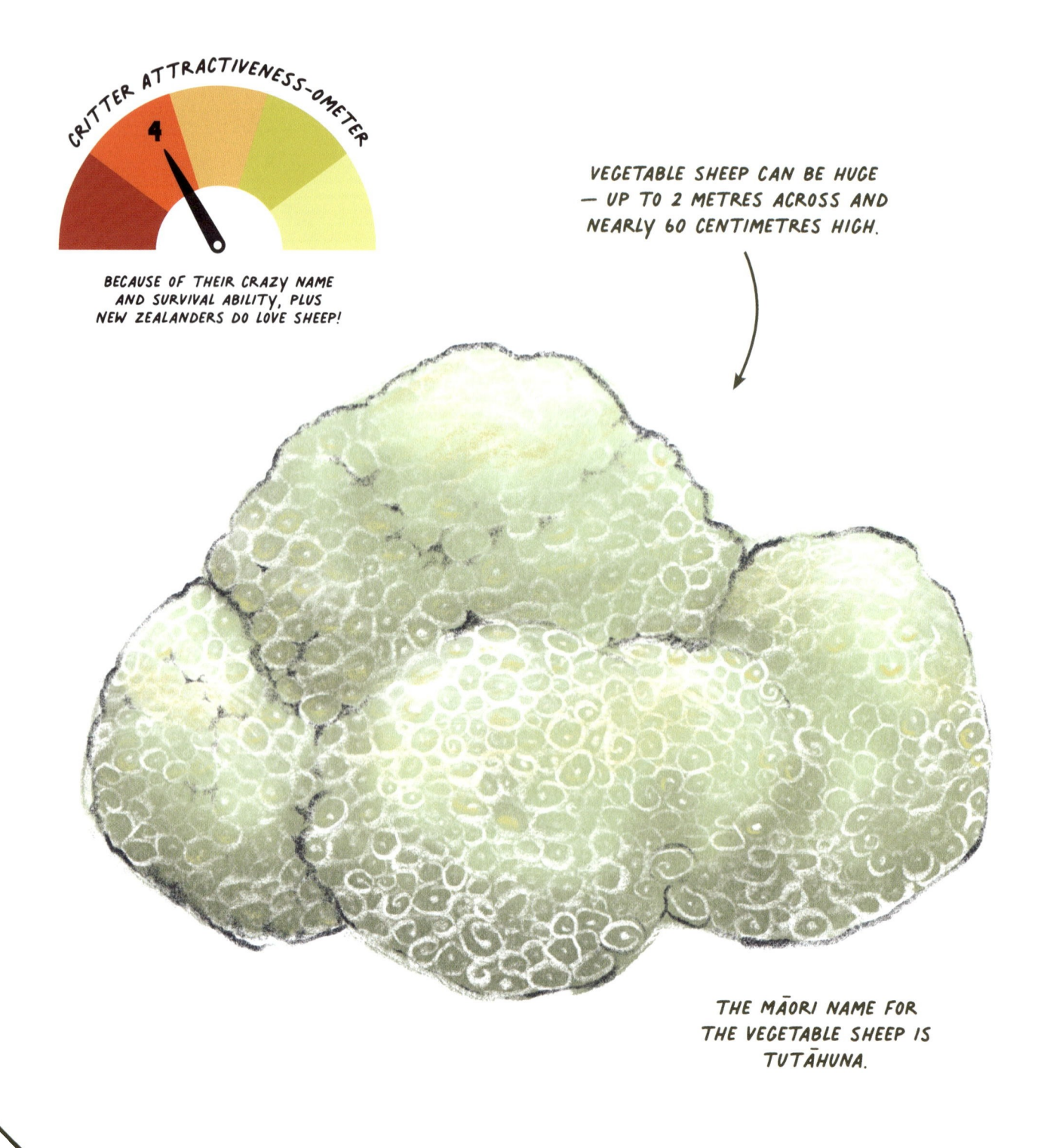

4

BECAUSE OF THEIR CRAZY NAME AND SURVIVAL ABILITY, PLUS NEW ZEALANDERS DO LOVE SHEEP!

VEGETABLE SHEEP CAN BE HUGE — UP TO 2 METRES ACROSS AND NEARLY 60 CENTIMETRES HIGH.

THE MĀORI NAME FOR THE VEGETABLE SHEEP IS TUTĀHUNA.

VEGETABLE SHEEP

The vegetable sheep might surprise you, because it is not in fact a sheep, nor any other kind of animal. In fact, as the first part of its name might suggest, it is a very special plant. Any tramper, outdoorsperson or high-country farmer will recognise the name immediately, because they're ubiquitous in the subalpine landscape.

There are about 23 species of vegetable sheep, all in the genus *Raoulia*, and they are unique to Aotearoa. They were named vegetable sheep because they look like sheep in the landscape, but they are in fact a member of the daisy family — a daisy that has tiny little interlaced flowers. The plant then hooks together in a really robust fashion so that it looks like a sheep!

The best way to describe them is that they're really tightly compressed shrubs. It's kind of like when you take an old car to the wreckers and they squash it into a cube — that's essentially what a vegetable sheep is, a shrub that's been squished into a really dense space, in order to survive in extreme climatic conditions in an alpine environment.

They make really good 'waypoints' to navigate with in the alpine landscape. Some of the vegetable sheep that deer cullers used in the 1930s to help signpost where they were are still there today! And they still trick people — high-country farmers sometimes send their dogs to round them up when mustering their sheep!

Their longevity is associated with the way they live. They're self-composting: the inside rots to form a spongy peat, and the plant feeds on those nutrients to keep growing. They like to live on rocky ground, so you will find them on scree slopes, big boulder fields and cliff faces across Aotearoa, from the Tararua mountains to Rakiura/Stewart Island. The best survival strategy in some of those extreme environments is just to hang onto the ground as hard as you can and grow slowly.

Due to the dynamic nature of the environment they're found in, they face rockfalls, landslides and some pretty extreme weather — and the jury's still out on the impact of climate change. If you're something that takes a really long time to evolve and lives for a really long time, the fast-moving nature of climate change is probably going to present some challenges.

WANDERING SEA ANEMONE

The wandering sea anemone is known as hūmenga in Māori: 'hū' means to be sneaky or secret or stealthy; 'hume' means to tuck or gather up; and 'nga' means to kind of pull that all into action — which is a beaut description of *Phlyctenactis tuberculosa*.

Wandering sea anemones are browny red or browny green, and have a magnificent thicket of tentacles around one end. And they're not small — they can grow to a maximum size of 15 centimetres in diameter, and 25 centimetres long.

They look like they've got a very bad case of warts. These little 'warts' are actually bladder-like pockets of air, almost like bubble-wrap, on their surface. They use these to operate their buoyancy and move up and down through the water column. If a predator tries to grab them, they can use that same pressure to shrink down so that they can escape.

The other very cool thing about them is when you stick your finger in an anemone and it feels like your finger is stuck to it, you're experiencing micro-harpoons called nematocysts. Like jellyfish, anemones have these amazing cells which are essentially a tiny little harpoon that shoots out of the cell and fires into whatever has touched it. Nematocysts do contain venom, but because we're so massive in comparison, the little harpoons don't even penetrate our skin.

Most anemones just stick to a rock and stay there, waving their tentacles around to catch things — but this anemone is a traveller, so they wander around finding food while they're on the road.

Anemones usually reproduce asexually — that means they don't need a partner to have babies, they just bud off another anemone. It's like if you just grew another head out of your shoulder that eventually grew into another entire person, who then broke off and wandered away! Or they have what's called 'pedal laceration', which means that as it's wandering around it might accidentally leave a bit of its foot behind — and that just turns into a new anemone! We as humans fall into the trap of thinking that evolution has finished with us, but we can't do anything as cool as that yet.

They are also quite fragile, so remember, if you're poking around in rockpools, always be gentle with them.

CRITTER ATTRACTIVENESS-OMETER — 7

BECAUSE IT'S LIKE AN UNDERWATER FLOWER THAT WALKS AROUND, WARTS AND ALL!

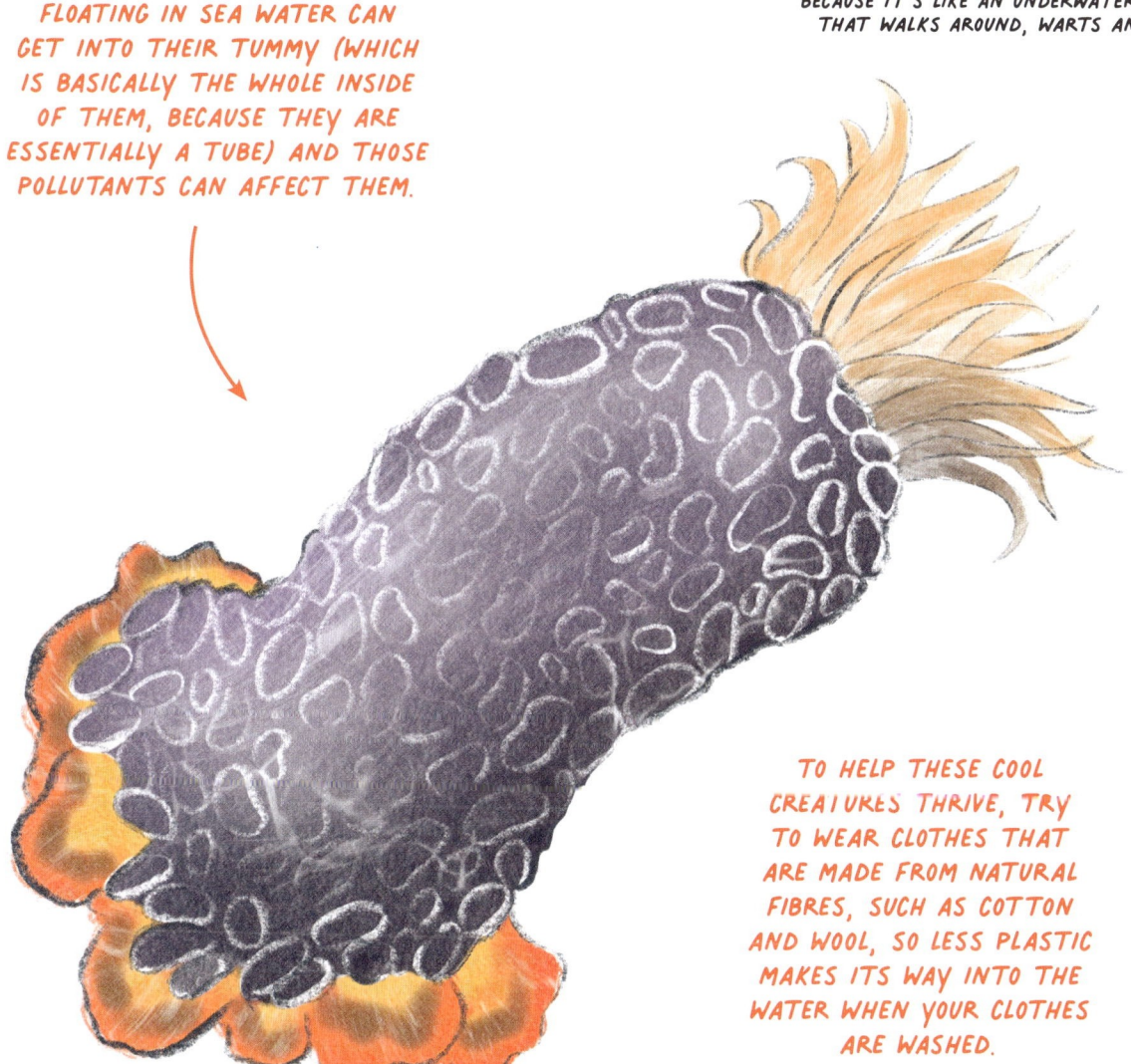

ONE ISSUE FOR ANEMONES IS MICROPLASTICS. MICROPLASTICS FLOATING IN SEA WATER CAN GET INTO THEIR TUMMY (WHICH IS BASICALLY THE WHOLE INSIDE OF THEM, BECAUSE THEY ARE ESSENTIALLY A TUBE) AND THOSE POLLUTANTS CAN AFFECT THEM.

TO HELP THESE COOL CREATURES THRIVE, TRY TO WEAR CLOTHES THAT ARE MADE FROM NATURAL FIBRES, SUCH AS COTTON AND WOOL, SO LESS PLASTIC MAKES ITS WAY INTO THE WATER WHEN YOUR CLOTHES ARE WASHED.

OVER WINTER, WRYBILLS GATHER IN HUGE FLOCKS WHICH FLY IN CO-ORDINATED MANOEUVRES THAT LOOK LIKE A SCARF BEING THROWN IN THE AIR.

WRYBILLS HAVE GOOD CAMOUFLAGE AND USE DISTRACTION TO COPE WITH PREDATORS. THEY MAY PRETEND TO HAVE A BROKEN WING TO LEAD ATTACKERS AWAY FROM THEIR NESTS OR CHICKS.

CRITTER ATTRACTIVENESS-OMETER
7.7

THESE ARE SPECIAL TO NIC BECAUSE SHE SEES THEM ON BEACHES AND BY BRAIDED RIVERS IN CANTERBURY, WHERE SHE LIVES.

WRYBILL / NGUTU PARE / NGUTU PARORE

These are amazing wee birds. They're the only bird in the world with a bill that curves sideways, always to the right.

They're a really interesting bird, because they migrate internally — within New Zealand. In spring they hang out on the beaches near the ends of braided rivers in the South Island, then they fly inland and breed in places such as the Mackenzie Basin or up the rivers like the upper Rangitata and Rakaia, then in winter they migrate to more northerly beaches like Miranda in the Firth of Thames.

They work along the edges of the braided rivers, collecting little invertebrates from underneath the stones. When they're feeding on these very small creatures, the birds can scrape their bills back and forth about a hundred times a minute.

These birds like to live on the little islands in the middle of braided rivers, and they need to clear a space to lay their tiny little eggs in tiny little dips in the stones. When we take too much water out of the rivers and the water level goes down, these islands fill up with weeds, like lupin and broom, and become great places for pests, like feral cats, hedgehogs and ferrets, to hide in.

We think there's only about 5000 wrybills left (about the same size of population as kea). Wrybill get preyed on by introduced mammals — we've lost a lot of wrybills to predation, including hedgehogs snaffling their eggs (bad, bad hedgehogs)! Their tiny eggs are also really hard to see among the stones. People who hoon around on our braided river beds in four-wheel-drives or motorbikes are a big threat.

In addition to nesting in braided rivers, wrybill have been seen trying to make a go of nesting on the tarmac at Auckland Airport — not very wise. And, unfortunately, when they're in areas with lots of man-made structures, they tend to prang into them and come off second-best.

Quite often little shorebirds or wading birds are quite hard to get close to, but you can get close to wrybills as long as you're quiet and careful, so you can sit and watch what they do. They're fascinating! And when the wee chicks come out looking like little grey bumblebees, they're so cute.

YELLOW OCTOPUS

There's something about octopuses that makes them endlessly fascinating. They are super-intelligent, despite being a mollusc — their closest relatives are snails, slugs and shellfish.

Octopuses are great escape artists. Some years ago, there was one at the Portobello aquarium in Dunedin that would regularly escape out of its tank at night. Octopuses can get through tiny places; by squishing their bodies right down so they can squeeze through a gap as small as 1 centimetre. This octopus would go out of its tank into the next tank (which just happened to be full of crayfish), eat everything in there, then squeeze back into its own tank. In the morning, he'd just be sitting there innocently but with a very full octopus belly!

Yellow octopus, *Enteroctopus zealandicus*, are both amazing and enormous — they can grow up to 1.4 metres long! They live down about 200–300 metres below the surface in the Southern Ocean (including the Chatham Rise). We know that they are a really important food source for the New Zealand sea lion, which are estimated to eat a million of them each year, but scientists have only ever found 50 specimens! Every time scientists try to catch them to learn more about them, these octopuses outwit them.

In 2016, a team from NIWA went to the subantarctic Auckland Islands to survey what the New Zealand sea lions were eating. They knew that the trawl nets weren't working to catch octopuses — the octopuses kept climbing out of them — so they designed a very special octopus trap, made of two pipes about 1-metre long. The thinking behind it was that yellow octopuses would make a home inside these traps — but in total they only caught one octopus, and it escaped as they were pulling it up!

They're so intelligent, yet there's still so much left to learn about them — we don't even know much about what they eat or where they live.

Once you've hung out with an octopus, you're probably never going to want to eat one again!

WE KNOW THEY CAN BE QUITE PLAYFUL AND MISCHIEVOUS, AND THAT THEY'RE GOOD PARENTS. SOMETIMES THEY WILL TAKE A YEAR OFF — NOT EVEN EATING — TO LOOK AFTER THEIR EGGS.

CRITTER ATTRACTIVENESS-OMETER: 8

POINTS FOR INTELLIGENCE AND ALSO FOR BEING NIC'S FAVOURITE COLOUR.

THERE ARE AROUND 40 SPECIES OF OCTOPUS FOUND IN NEW ZEALAND WATERS, ALTHOUGH MOST PEOPLE ENCOUNTER ONLY THOSE THAT LIVE IN SHALLOW COASTAL WATERS.

CRITTER ATTRACTIVENESS-OMETER

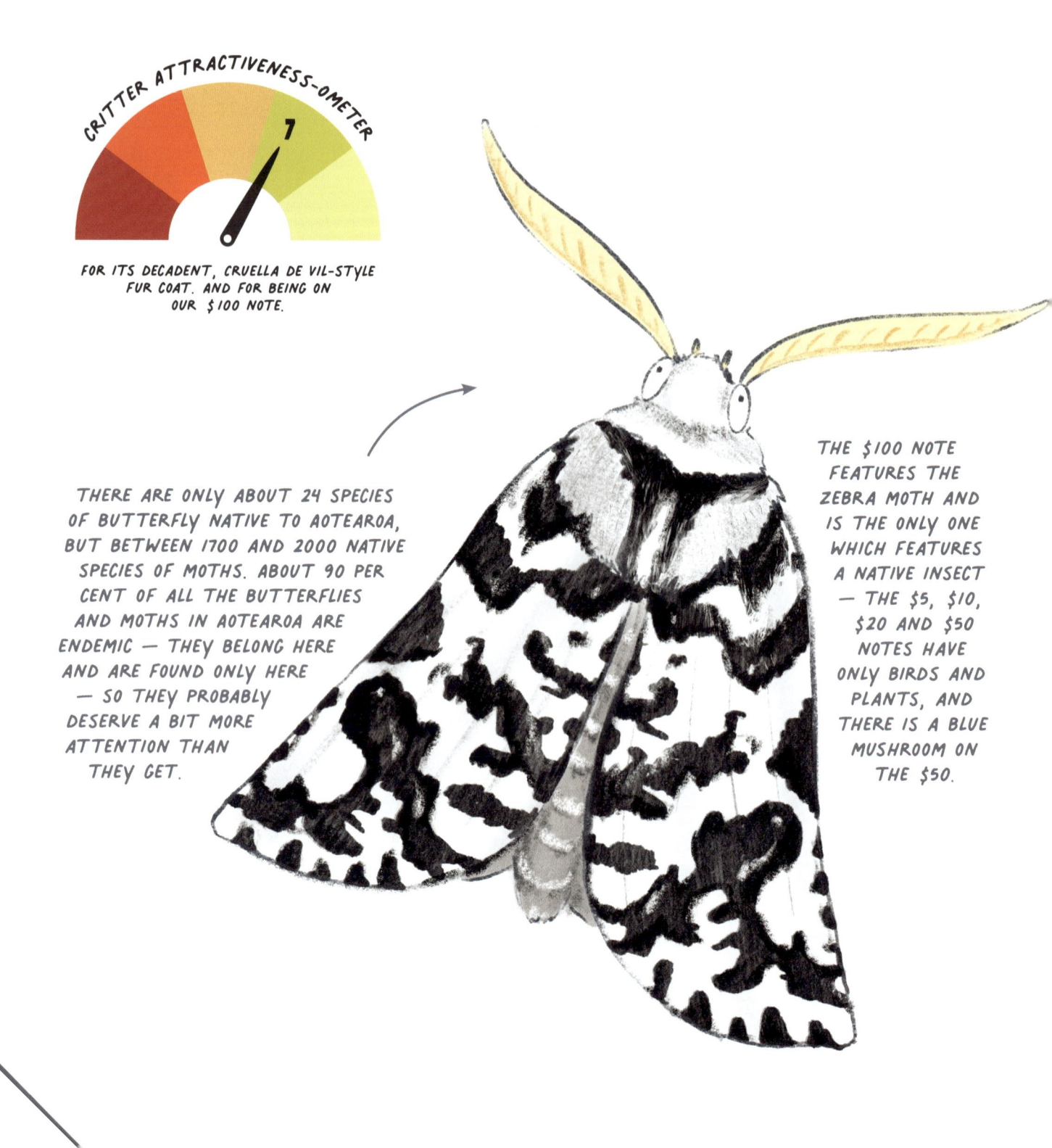

7

FOR ITS DECADENT, CRUELLA DE VIL-STYLE FUR COAT. AND FOR BEING ON OUR $100 NOTE.

THERE ARE ONLY ABOUT 24 SPECIES OF BUTTERFLY NATIVE TO AOTEAROA, BUT BETWEEN 1700 AND 2000 NATIVE SPECIES OF MOTHS. ABOUT 90 PER CENT OF ALL THE BUTTERFLIES AND MOTHS IN AOTEAROA ARE ENDEMIC — THEY BELONG HERE AND ARE FOUND ONLY HERE — SO THEY PROBABLY DESERVE A BIT MORE ATTENTION THAN THEY GET.

THE $100 NOTE FEATURES THE ZEBRA MOTH AND IS THE ONLY ONE WHICH FEATURES A NATIVE INSECT — THE $5, $10, $20 AND $50 NOTES HAVE ONLY BIRDS AND PLANTS, AND THERE IS A BLUE MUSHROOM ON THE $50.

ZEBRA MOTH / SOUTH ISLAND LICHEN MOTH

This little moth, with the scientific name *Declana egregia*, is quite beautiful. They're featured on our $100 note. In real life, they kind of look like they're wearing a little fur coat!

Unlike butterflies, which tend to have little knobs on the ends of their antennae and fold their wings vertically up behind them, moths have lovely, big, feathery antennae — that scientists think detect vibrations and chemical messengers called pheromones — and they don't tend to fold up their wings in the same way. Most moths fly around at night, although there are quite a lot of species that spend time flying during the day — just to confuse things — and there are species of butterfly that look more like moths, and vice versa.

This particular moth lives at higher altitudes, in forest areas. Its caterpillars look like brown twigs or bird poo, so they can be quite hard to spot — a pretty good plan if you're avoiding predators!

To find the moths themselves you'll need to look in the lichen on the trees, because that's what they eat. And they're pretty well camouflaged, so you're going to need to be looking at that lichen very closely!

One troubling thing about moths in New Zealand is that a lot of them are confined to living off one food source (one plant or, in the case of one species of moth, the dung of the endangered short-tailed bat), so if the food species (e.g. the bat) gets in trouble, then the other species (the moth) gets in trouble too.

The different varieties of moth species can help scientists work out the story of continental drift, based on what we can see in the evolutionary path of moths and butterflies in New Zealand. This science is known as paleogeology. A lot of scientists in Aotearoa use plants and animals to help tell that story, but moths are useful because we have such a huge variety of them, so we can get a much more detailed picture of exactly what happened.

CRITTER QUIZ

HOW WELL DO YOU KNOW YOUR CRITTERS OF AOTEAROA?
TEST YOUR SKILLS, THEN CHECK YOUR ANSWERS ON PAGE 119.

1. WHICH OF THESE CRITTERS FLIES THOUSANDS OF KILOMETRES IN THEIR LIFETIME BUT HAS NO WINGS?

1.

2.

3.

4.

2. WHICH OF THESE CRITTERS WAS NAMED AFTER A CHARACTER FROM J.R.R. TOLKIEN'S <u>THE LORD OF THE RINGS</u>?

1

2

3

4

CROSSWORD

DOWN

1. THE LONG-TAILED BAT IS ALSO KNOWN AS: _____

2. THIS CRITTER LIVES IN COMPLETE DARKNESS, MORE THAN 1 KILOMETRE BELOW THE SURFACE OF THE OCEAN: _____

3. THE TEVIOT FLATHEAD GALAXIAS IS A TYPE OF: ____

5. THE _____ SPIDER HAS A POISONOUS BITE.

6. THE _____ MOTH IS FEATURED ON NEW ZEALAND'S $100 NOTE.

ACROSS

4. THIS CRITTER IS A GREAT ESCAPE ARTIST: _____

7. THESE 'WATER BEARS' ARE REALLY FUN TO LOOK AT WITH A MICROSCOPE: _____

8. THESE GRUBS SUPPOSEDLY TASTE LIKE PEANUT BUTTER: ____

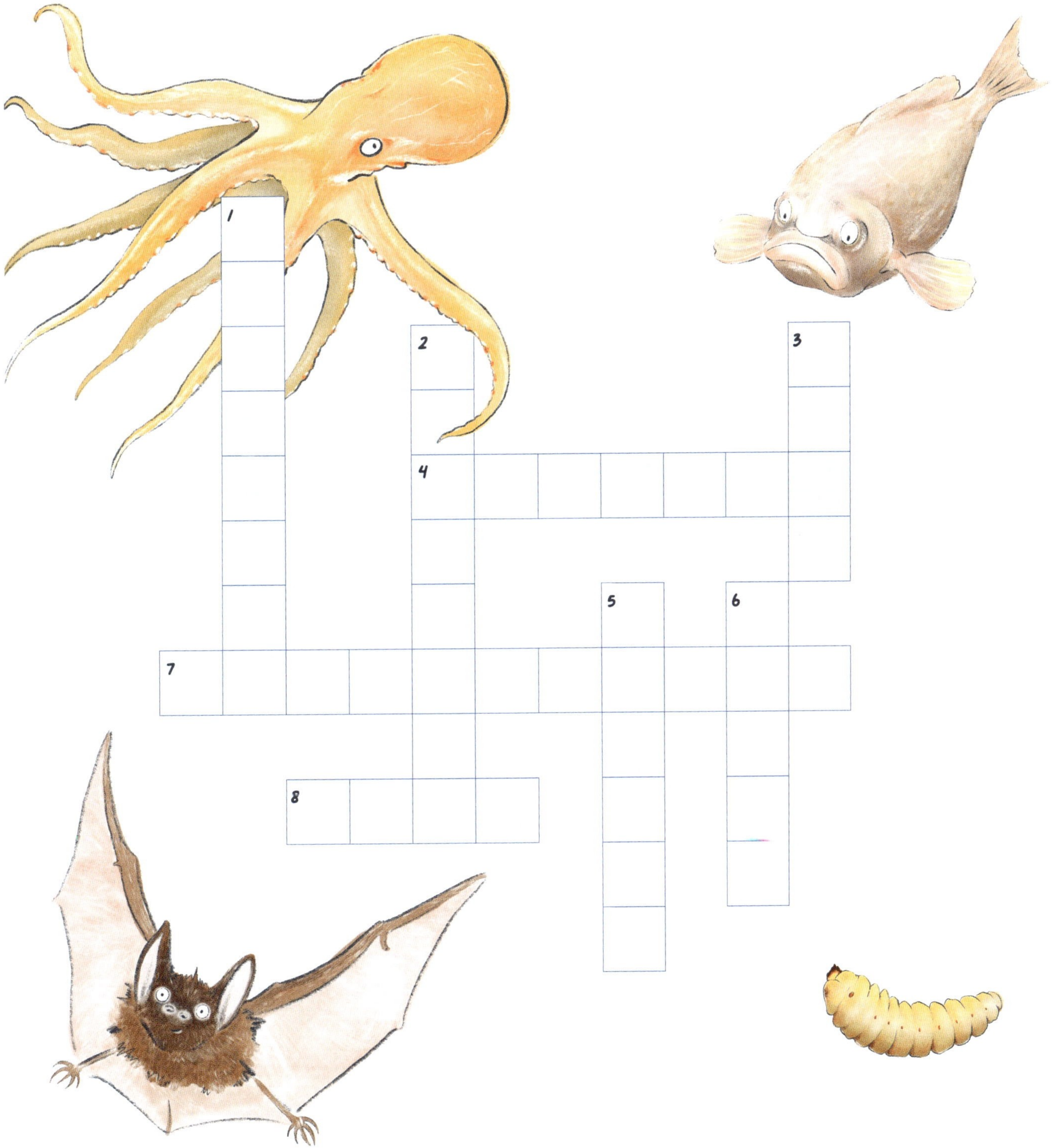
1
2
3
4
5
6
7
8

WORDFIND

THERE ARE 23 CRITTER-THEMED WORDS
HIDING ON THE OPPOSITE PAGE.
CAN YOU FIND THEM ALL?

PARAKEET	SNAIL	GLOW WORM
FROG	GECKO	LAMPREY
WHALE	BEETLE	NUDIBRANCH
CICADA	MOTH	GRASSHOPPER
DOG VOMIT	SLUG	SKINK
SLIME MOULD	SHRIMP	MAGGOT
WEEVIL	ANTLION	ANEMONE
LIMPET	CRICKET	

G	M	R	O	W	W	O	L	G	D	E	S	D	T
R	G	T	E	K	C	I	R	C	N	I	L	O	E
E	M	A	G	G	O	T	S	O	U	R	I	G	P
P	I	L	H	T	O	M	H	T	D	B	M	V	M
P	A	P	I	C	E	I	R	E	I	E	E	O	I
O	C	I	C	A	D	A	I	E	B	E	M	M	L
H	A	W	S	S	N	N	M	K	R	T	O	I	V
S	N	N	E	O	A	S	P	A	A	L	U	T	Y
S	T	O	E	E	I	K	H	R	N	E	L	S	E
A	S	G	I	M	V	M	O	A	C	E	D	S	R
R	G	O	E	L	O	I	O	P	H	L	K	K	P
G	L	R	T	C	T	N	L	K	S	A	S	I	M
R	R	F	E	O	K	N	E	V	O	H	E	N	A
S	L	U	G	E	O	O	A	M	O	W	O	K	L

INDEX

AMPHIBIANS
Archey's Frog 10–11

BIRDS
Antipodes Island Parakeet 8–9
Marsh Crake / Koitareke 56–57
Wrybill / Ngutu Pare / Ngutu Parore 102–103

CRUSTACEANS
Mantis Shrimp 54–55
New Zealand Pea Crab 68–69
Tadpole Shrimp / Shield Shrimp 90–91

FISH
Blobfish 12–13
Hagfish 34–35
Longfin Eel / Tuna 52–53
New Zealand Lamprey 66–67
Teviot Flathead Galaxias 96–97

FUNGI
Dog Vomit Slime Mould 22–23
Tea-Tree Fingers 94–95

INSECTS
Cicadas / Kihikihi / Tātarakihi 16–17
Cook Strait Giant Wētā 18–19
Forest Ringlet Butterfly 24–25
Giant Knobbled Weevil 28–29
Helms' Stag Beetle 38–39
Horrid Stick Insect 40–41
Huhu 42–43
Kupe's Grass Moth 46–47
Mercury Islands Tusked Wētā 58–59
Native Mole Cricket 60–61
New Zealand Antlion / Kutu Kutu 62–63
New Zealand Glow Worm 64–65
Robust Grasshopper 76–77
Seabird Tick 78–79
Zebra Moth / South Island Lichen Moth 106–107

INVERTEBRATES
Crimson Jellyfish 20–21
Freshwater Bristle Worm 26–27
Glow-in-the-Dark Freshwater Snail Limpet 30–31
Greta Thunberg Freshwater Snail 32–33
Leaf-Veined Slug 48–49
Nudibranchs 70–71
Peripatus / Ngāokeoke / Velvet Worm / Walking Worm 72–73
Sea Squirt or Sea Tulip / Kaeo 80–81
Smeagol the Gravel Maggot 86–87
Wandering Sea Anemone 100–101
Yellow Octopus 104–105

MAMMALS
Bryde's Whale 14–15
Long-Tailed Bat 50–51

MOLLUSCS
see Invertebrates

PLANTS
Vegetable Sheep 98–99

REPTILES
Harlequin Gecko 36–37
Sinbad Skink 82–83
Striped Skink 88–89

SPIDERS
Katipō Spider 44–45
Rangatira Spider 74–75
Six-Eyed Spider 84–85

???
Tardigrades 92–93

ATTRACTIVENESS INDEX

(Critters ordered from lowest attractiveness-ometer rating to highest)

EW, YUCK!

New Zealand Lamprey 66–67
Hagfish 34–35
Seabird Tick 78–79
Smeagol the Gravel Maggot 86–87
Leaf-Veined Slug 48–49
Blobfish 12–13
Tea-Tree Fingers 94–95
Sea Squirt or Sea Tulip / Kaeo 80–81

NO, THANK YOU.

Dog Vomit Slime Mould 22–23
Freshwater Bristle Worm 26–27
Huhu Grub 42
Greta Thunberg Freshwater Snail 32–33
Kupe's Grass Moth 46–47
Marsh Crake / Koitareke 56–57
Tadpole Shrimp / Shield Shrimp 90–91
Teviot Flathead Galaxias 96–97
Vegetable Sheep 98–99

NOT BAD, NOT BAD.

Native Mole Cricket 60–61
New Zealand Pea Crab 68–69
Robust Grasshopper 76–77
Cicadas / Kihikihi / Tātarakihi 16–17
Giant Knobbled Weevil 28–29
Horrid Stick Insect 40–41
Huhu Beetle 43
New Zealand Antlion / Kutu Kutu 62–63

ALRIGHT, I GUESS.

Rangatira Spider 74–75
Striped Skink 88–89
Tardigrades 92–93
Wandering Sea Anemone 100–101
Zebra Moth / South Island Lichen Moth 106–107
Glow-in-the-Dark Freshwater Snail Limpet 30–31
Forest Ringlet Butterfly 24–25
Antipodes Island Parakeet 8–9
Katipō Spider 44–45
Wrybill / Ngutu Pare / Ngutu Parore 102–103
Long-Tailed Bat 50–51
New Zealand Glow Worm 64–65
Helms' Stag Beetle 38–39
Archey's Frog 10–11
Cook Strait Giant Wētā 18–19
Mantis Shrimp 54–55
Sinbad Skink 82–83

Yellow Octopus 104–105
Bryde's Whale 14–15
Mercury Islands Tusked Wētā 58–59
Nudibranchs 70–71
Peripatus / Ngāokeoke / Velvet Worm / Walking Worm 72–73
Six-Eyed Spider 84–85

WOW, SO ATTRACTIVE!

Harlequin Gecko 36–37
Longfin Eel / Tuna 52–53
Crimson Jellyfish 20–21

ABOUT NIC

Nicola Toki has been a 'nature nerd' for as long as she can remember. She is deeply passionate about Aotearoa New Zealand's endemic wildlife, and especially telling stories about it to anyone who will listen!

As a kid, Nic had tadpoles, caterpillars and praying mantises as pets, and likely drove her parents mad with her collection of things she found on the beach — including her prized dried stinky shark's head and a penguin carcass.

After studying zoology and natural history filmmaking at the University of Otago (which led her to spend a summer on an island near the Antarctic Peninsula researching Adelie penguins), Nic feels very lucky to have built a career as a champion for nature. She believes that telling people stories of hope drives action to protect the species we love. Nic hopes we can create more nature lovers by focusing on fun and pointing out the whimsy in the natural world.

Nic lives in North Canterbury with her husband Chris, son Hunter and a collection of 'wildlife', including Bess the dog, Topaz the tiny horse, a handful of sinister chickens and a born-to-be-wild cat called Pango (don't ask!) who slinks in most evenings for a meal he doesn't appreciate.

ABOUT LILY

Lily Duval is an artist, writer and researcher based in beautiful Ōhinehou/Lyttelton. She's an insect nerd, book lover and obsessive tramper.

Lily's always been addicted to drawing — in kindergarten the teachers had to pull her away from the paints so the other children could have a turn! A love of stories led her to complete a Masters in English Literature, which examined our attitudes to insects here in Aotearoa. She's always raving about why we need to love bugs and not squish them.

This is her first picture book.

ACKNOWLEDGEMENTS

'Critter of the Week' was born when, while working for the Department of Conservation, I was asked to do a radio interview about corporate sponsorship of wildlife in New Zealand. I heard myself use phrases such as 'leveraging synergies' and I realised the interviewer, Jesse Mulligan, was bored. So I blurted out 'Look, Jesse, the problem is that in New Zealand everyone loves a "K" bird. Everyone wants to sponsor a kea or a kākā or a kākāpō, but nobody cares about Smeagol the gravel maggot.' When I put the phone down, it immediately rang again, and Jesse's producer Bridget asked if I could come on every week. That was almost a decade ago. Thanks to Jesse for loving 'the nature' as much as me.

Thanks also to the RNZ listeners, who continue to stop me in the street to tell me how much they love Critter. Thanks to Margaret (of Penguin Random House) for reaching out and asking whether our rambling (and sometimes wildly inappropriate) radio yarns could be formatted into a book, and to Grace for interpreting them.

To the very talented Lily, for bringing these critters to life on paper — you're a legend.

A big kia ora to Mike Dickinson and the Wikipedia-behind-the-scenes Critter crew for amplifying the science behind the stories.

And a huge thanks to my whānau for supporting me along the Critter journey and while working on this book — and for everything else!

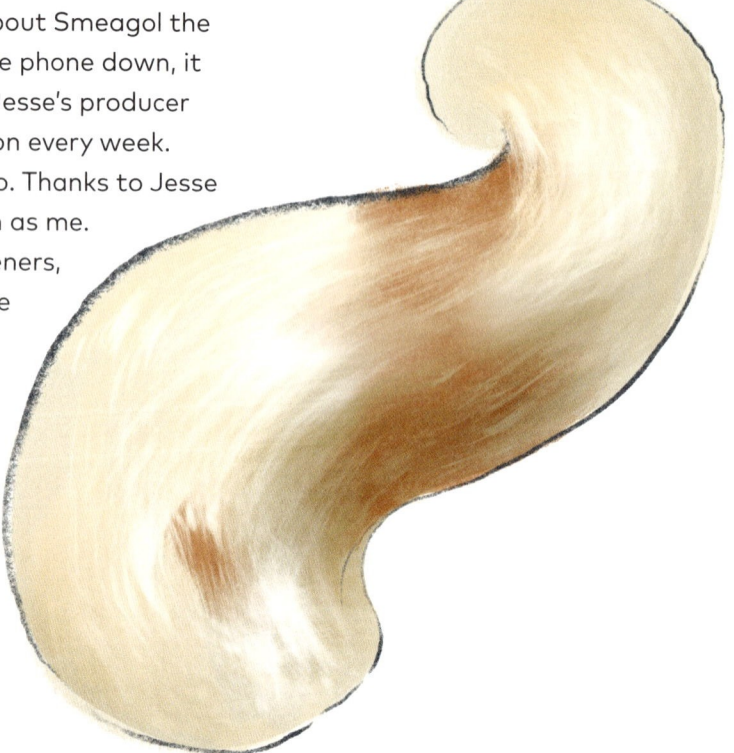

ANSWERS

Question 1 (page 108): Seabird tick #4

Question 2 (page 109): Smeagol the gravel maggot #2

Crossword (pages 110–11)

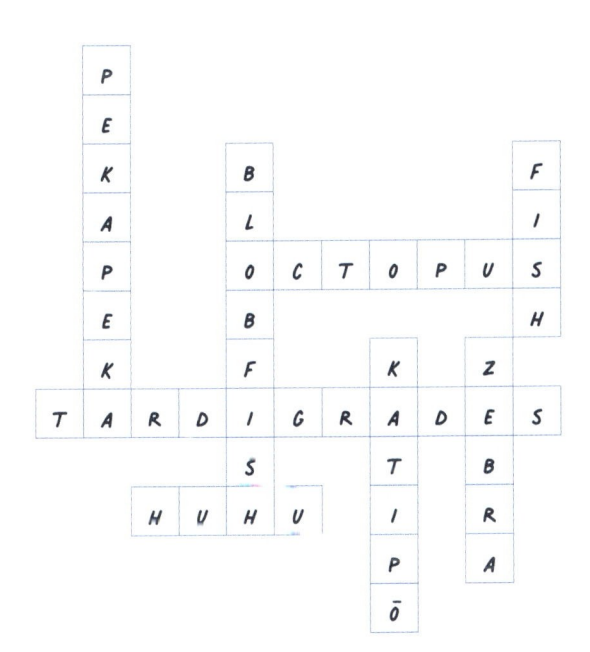

	P										
	E										
	K			B						F	
	A			L						I	
	P			O	C	T	O	P	U	S	
	E			B						H	
	K			F			K		Z		
T	A	R	D	I	G	R	A	D	E	S	
				S			T		B		
		H	U	H	U		I		R		
							P		A		
							Ō				

Wordfind (pages 112–13)

G	M	R	O	W	W	O	L	G	D	E	S	D	T
R	G	T	E	K	C	I	R	C	N	I	L	O	E
E	M	A	G	G	O	T	S	O	U	R	I	G	P
P	I	L	H	T	O	M	H	T	D	B	M	V	M
P	A	P	I	C	E	I	R	E	I	E	E	O	I
O	C	I	C	A	D	A	I	E	B	E	M	M	L
H	A	W	S	S	N	N	M	K	R	T	O	I	V
S	N	N	E	O	A	S	P	A	A	L	U	T	Y
S	T	O	E	E	I	K	H	R	N	E	L	S	E
A	S	G	I	M	V	M	O	A	C	E	D	S	R
R	G	O	E	L	O	I	O	P	H	L	K	K	P
G	L	R	T	C	T	N	L	K	S	A	S	I	M
R	P	F	E	O	K	N	E	V	O	H	E	N	A
S	L	U	G	E	O	O	A	M	O	W	O	K	I

TO MY FAVOURITE CRITTER, HUNTER MANAIA, WHO LOVES LEARNING ABOUT NATURE AS MUCH I DO. — NT

FOR ALL THE CRITTERS AND THE PEOPLE WHO CARE FOR THEM. — LD

PUFFIN

UK | USA | Canada | Ireland | Australia
India | New Zealand | South Africa | China

Puffin is an imprint of the Penguin Random House group of companies, whose addresses can be found at global.penguinrandomhouse.com.

Penguin Random House New Zealand

RNZ TE REO IRIRANGI O AOTEAROA

First published by Penguin Random House New Zealand, 2023

1 3 5 7 9 10 8 6 4 2

Text © Nicola Toki, 2023
Illustrations © Lily Duval, 2023

The moral right of the author has been asserted.

All rights reserved. Without limiting the rights under copyright reserved above, no part of this publication may be reproduced, stored in or introduced into a retrieval system, or transmitted, in any form or by any means (electronic, mechanical, photocopying, recording or otherwise), without the prior written permission of both the copyright owner and the above publisher of this book.

Design by Cat Taylor © Penguin Random House New Zealand
Prepress by Soar Communications Group
Printed and bound in China by RR Donnelley
Produced using vegetable-based inks.

A catalogue record for this book is available from the National Library of New Zealand.

ISBN 978-1-77695-802-3

penguin.co.nz

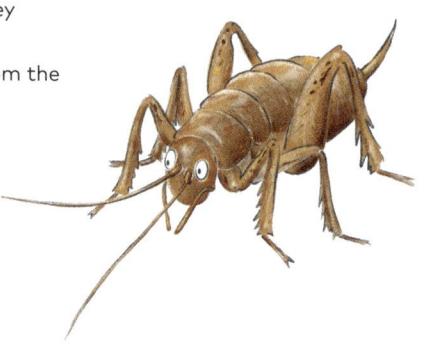

MIX
Paper | Supporting responsible forestry
FSC® C144853